DATE DUE

09 R Js.	
6-09 URC	
7-09 Arnold	

HAMMER OF GOD

Deputy Joe Hammer always gets his man. Thugs and killers don't give in easy: most are brought in slung over a saddle. Seeking a peaceful life, he resigns his badge, hangs up his guns and rides south to Mexico. But when Joe's friends are gunned down by Gomez Farias, the Hammer of God is roused. As a former lawman, the blood that flowed was a trickle compared to the flood unleashed when Joe rides out on the vengeance trail.

Books by P. McCormac
in the Linford Western Library:

MASSACRE AT EMPIRE FASTNESS

P. McCORMAC

HAMMER OF GOD

Complete and Unabridged

LINFORD
Leicester

First published in Great Britain in 2007 by
Robert Hale Limited
London

First Linford Edition
published 2009
by arrangement with
Robert Hale Limited
London

British Library CIP Data

McCormac, P.
  Hammer of God- -(Linford western library)
  1. Western stories.
  2. Large type books.
  I. Title II. Series
  823.9'2–dc22

  ISBN 978–1–84782–661–9

Published by
F. A. Thorpe (Publishing)
Anstey, Leicestershire

Set by Words & Graphics Ltd.
Anstey, Leicestershire
Printed and bound in Great Britain by
T. J. International Ltd., Padstow, Cornwall

PART ONE

THE HAMMER CRUMBLES

How is the hammer of the whole earth cut asunder and broken!

Jeremiah 50:3

1

The carrion birds had spotted the man lying motionless in the creek bed. He lay face up with no sign of life. The vultures traced intricate patterns in the sky as they hovered and eyed with anticipation the feast to come. Like the vultures the man was garbed in sombre colours: black wool shirt and black cord trousers. A black, low-crowned hat lay a short distance from his supine figure. As if to offset all the black, his untidy hair was the colour of ripening wheat. The hair was long and the loose strands spilled like threads of gold over the dull stones in the dried-up creek bed.

Around his waist could be seen a gunbelt with a holstered Colt. He was a tall man and seemed lean. On closer inspection the appearance of leanness was an illusion. His shirt stretched tightly across heavily muscled shoulders and upper arms. His outflung arm ended in a broad wrist and long powerful fingers. Blood leaked from an ugly bullet graze on his right temple. The buzzards dropped lower and lower.

There was a movement to the left of the creek bed and a man appeared out of the shrub. At this sign of activity the carrion birds drifted higher. The newcomer stepped cautiously making no sound as he moved. He held a rifle at the ready. Two more men appeared and exercising the same caution followed him. They were carrying pistols. At the edge of the creek the three halted, and stared down at the supine figure.

'Jake, you sure done for that lousy lawman.'

The man with the rifle let go the stock of his weapon and held it loosely by the barrel. He was a tall, skinny man with a straggly beard.

'Ain't much I cain't hit that I aim at,' he said. 'Whet my milk teeth on a

4

Winchester. My old man had me out hunting possum and squirrels from when I was knee-high to a goat's balls. Get his weapons.'

The two youngsters were so alike there was no doubt they were brothers. The trio were dressed in heavy twill trousers and loose fitting cotton shirts. One of the brothers stepped into the creek bed and snatched the Colt from the man in black.

'I reckon I'll have that there star.' As he plucked at the deputy's badge the man moaned and moved slightly. 'Goddamn varmint's still alive.'

The youngster got rapidly to his feet. He cocked and pointed his gun at the injured lawman but held his fire as the bearded, skinny man called out:

'Hang on there. If'n he ain't daid we can have some entertainment. Drag him out of there an' git a fire started. We'll have us some fun. See if'n we cain't wake him up.'

* * *

He became dimly aware of the throbbing pain in his head. Somewhere inside his cranium a small devil was banging on his skull with a wooden mallet. There were voices as well. He did not think the voices were in his head. He tried to figure out where he was.

'Git his boots off.'

He could smell wood smoke.

'A hot iron on the feet always wakes 'em. I got me a piece of copper wire in my saddle-bag — a rustler's best tool. Changed more brands with that little ol' wire than I changed my pants. I'll go an' fetch that while you boys git him ready.'

His lids lifted slightly. There were three of them. The shadowy figure of the speaker moved out of sight. Another man was crouched by the fire feeding sticks to get the blaze going. A burly young man loomed over him and moved to his feet. He felt the hands grip his boot. Then the tugging began. The pain in his head was worse now but memory was returning.

I must be slipping, he thought as he lay on the ground with the top of his head threatening to separate from his skull and one of the rustlers tugging at his boot. His horse had stumbled as it picked its way across the cobbles of the creek bed. He had swayed in the saddle and wrenched at the reins. The bullet had bounced off his skull and he had known no more.

As the rustler pulled at his boot the deputy brought up his other foot and kicked the youngster in the mouth. With a startled yell he fell sideways. Deputy Joe Hammer went rolling into the youngster. A violent throbbing flared in his head at the sudden movement. Ignoring the pain he fell on top of the rustler. Out of the corner of his eye he saw the one by the fire rising and at the same time clawing for a gun.

The deputy plucked at the holstered gun belonging to the man he had downed. Shots winged past him. He tried to ignore them. Before he could free the holstered gun, hands were grasping at his clothing as the downed rustler began to fight back.

A bullet nicked the deputy's shoulder. The rustler by the fire was firing high for fear of hitting his brother. With desperate force the deputy swung the youngster up and over. The youth yelled but held on to the lawman's shirt. Bullets ceased to fly as the other youngster hesitated, fearful of hitting his brother who was now between him and his target.

In spite of the light-headedness and the pounding pain the deputy held grimly on to his living shield. One hand was gripping the butt of his attacker's revolver which he had failed to pull from the holster. Swivelling the body of his attacker he tipped the holstered gun upwards and emptied the six-shooter in the general direction of the second rustler. The youngster by the fire suddenly gave a grunt and staggered back. His hands clasped at his stomach.

'Goddamn it, Walt, I bin shot,' he

screamed. With a sudden movement he sat down, gazing in horror at the blood oozing through his fingers. 'Walt, help me,' he cried out in plaintive tones.

Walt was in no position to help as he was still grappling with the deputy.

'Goddamn lousy lawman, you shot Alf,' he yelled.

The deputy let go his grip on the now empty Colt still snared in the rustler's holster. He crashed his head into the face of the youngster. He almost passed out then as waves of red-hot agony pulsated through his head.

The youngster screamed and fought to get free. Blood was pouring freely from his busted nose. The deputy let go the youth, for his searching fingers had found the haft of the rustler's knife tucked into a sheath. As they separated and rolled away from each other the deputy kept a hold on the knife. The young rustler scrambled to his feet and snatched his Colt from the holster. His face was a twisted mask of blood and revenge as he pointed the weapon and pulled the trigger. The hammer rose and fell on already expended cartridges.

'Ask Alf where the bullets are,' gritted out the deputy.

His head was pounding and waves of dizziness swept over him as he managed to get to all fours. His opponent ran to his brother's side. The young rustler had keeled over and was weeping from the pain and fear of his injury. His revolver lay where he had dropped it. His brother was stooping for the weapon when the sudden explosion of the rifle halted him. Into view stalked the marksman with his deadly rifle.

'Make another move, lawman, an' you're dead.'

The deputy was on his feet but remained where he was, the knife hidden by his side.

'I'm gonna kill that sonabitch,' the young rustler screamed.

He had his brother's pistol in his hand and aimed deliberately at the deputy.

'Not yet, Walt,' yelled the rifleman, turning momentarily towards the youngster. It was a fatal distraction.

The handle of the purloined knife suddenly appeared in the man's throat. He gulped, then his mouth gaped in sudden agony. The wounded man put his hand to his throat and his fingers encountered the haft of the knife embedded in his neck. Like a man struggling for air his mouth worked feverishly. Blood stained his lips and he slowly knelt down, the rifle slanting towards the ground as his fingers slackened their grasp.

The lawman scrambled past the dying man towards the brothers. The man's shout had momentarily stayed the youngster's trigger finger. Seeing the deputy coming towards them he panicked and pulled the trigger. His hasty shots missed the fast-moving lawman.

The golden-haired man reached the young rustler. His clenched fist punched the boy hard in the face. The youth's nose, already busted by the deputy's head, splattered more blood on to his shirt. He screamed as he went down. The lawman walked unsteadily to the dead rifleman and found his own pistol. He holstered his gun, wrenched the rifle from lifeless fingers and turned back to the two youngsters. He was a fearsome sight with his blood-splattered face.

'Help me, Walt.' The cry was pathetic and weak.

The deputy looked at the youngster sitting on the ground holding blood-soaked hands to his midriff.

'Help your friend, Walt. I don't think he has the stomach for this fight no more.'

2

It was apparent to any observer: the six men, toughened by wind and rain and hard living, were dangerous.

Growler Gratten was so called because a bullet had lodged in his throat causing him to speak in a deep growl. His words were not always clear and only Gratten's closest comrades could make out what he was saying. Jesse Patterson was a big plain-faced man with muscular shoulders and spadelike hands. Then there was Pretty Boy Johnstone, living up to his name as a dandy.

His style of dress was flamboyant with silver-studded hat and vest. He wore crossed gunbelts, heavy with silver decoration. The youngest of the bunch was Kid Conachy — dark-haired and sallow-faced. He wore a thick black moustache on his upper lip and seldom smiled, looking out at the world as if he hated everyone out there.

Harry McDonald was the undisputed leader of the gang. Barely twenty years of age he was reputed to have killed a man for every year of his vicious life. Fair-haired and very handsome he was also uncommonly cold-blooded.

Somewhere along the line they had picked up Black Charley Jordan. That a black man should ride with this bunch was unusual. These men had all fought for the South in the bloody War between the States. Rumour was that Jordan and McDonald had grown up together back in Virginia. No one knew for sure and no one dared question the black man's presence in the gang.

The Wanted posters warned these men were extremely dangerous. It didn't need a wanted poster to point out the danger. The men themselves gave off an aura of menace — a barely suppressed violence lurking just beneath the surface. Meeting this pack was akin to stumbling upon a nest of rattlers. The difference was a rattler gave out its well-known warning. These men gave no warning of impending violence — often striking out without reason — leaving a bitter legacy of death and grief in their wake.

Heads came up as the noises came faintly through the sun-dried air. Indistinct at first, the sounds took a while to separate into the discord of people on the move: the distinct popping of a bullwhip, the faint shouts of men cussing the beasts that dragged their wagons and the faint rumble of wheels over the well-worn trail.

Horses stirred restlessly as the animals sensed the men's sudden alertness. The gang was well hidden from sight among the rocks and hardy shrubs that grew precariously in the boulder-strewn soil of the gorge. Guns were drawn and checked. Carbines were loosened in their saddle scabbards.

Colts were the favoured weapons among these hardy men. Most had spare guns tucked in waistbands or pockets. The habit of carrying extra weapons had begun during their stint in the North-South war. Prolonged battle situations required much shooting. It was easier to grab another loaded weapon than attempt to reload during a fight.

The noises from the wagons were getting louder. A rider on a dun horse came into view on the trail. He walked the horse easy so as not to draw too far ahead of the slow-moving wagons. He was the guide and hunter hired to take the wagons safely through inhospitable country. As well as acting as guide he would hunt for deer or buffalo, providing the wagon train with a supply of fresh meat.

The hidden watchers waited patiently as the guide drew level with them. Then the first wagon rumbled into sight. Still the gunmen waited. The guide turned in his saddle and glanced back. His bearded face was weather-beaten under a battered hat. He eased his horse to the side of the track and waited, looking relaxed and competent. Six pair of hard eyes watched the trail with him. He took out his carbine and rested it over the pummel of his saddle.

On came the wagons — iron-rimmed wheels rumbling over the beaten track where so many hopefuls had passed before. The hidden eyes automatically counted the number of wagons lumbering into view.

Two large oxen hauled the first wagon. The man in the driving seat yelled and swung his bullwhip, cussing the beasts. Beside him his wife sat prim-mouthed, plainly disapproving of his language. He had learned to cuss from his fellow travellers and it gave him perverse satisfaction to annoy his strait-laced consort by doing so.

'Goddamn whores, git them goddamn bloody carcasses moving! I'll cut your balls off and have them for breakfast.'

The cussing made no difference to the pace of the beasts. All it did cause a heated argument between husband and wife each stopover. 'Goddamn sons of bitches!' The whip popped out again.

They had almost drawn level with the guide waiting patiently by the side of the trail.

'Howdy, Jeb!' the driver yelled.

Behind him more wagons were strung out along the trail. The guide ignored the greeting. His carbine came up and he shot the leading ox in the head. The beast staggered, then bellowed. Again the carbine crashed out. This time the animal's legs suddenly gave way. It sagged in the harness. Its companion, startled by gunshots, plunged wildly in the traces.

'What the . . . ' began the startled driver as he hauled on the reins in a hopeless attempt to get some control. The wagon slewed to one side as the remaining ox lunged in a frenzied attempt to shake itself free.

The devils came out of the rocks then, screaming and firing at the wagons. They had learned to scream in the ranks of the Confederate infantry. It startled the enemy and unsettled green troops — the wild yelling along with the shooting was designed to confuse and terrify the opposition. The guide joined in the killing. He rode down the line putting bullets into men he had lived with over the past months.

It was over very quickly. Most of the men in the wagons were killed in the first savage attack. The few women who grabbed guns to defend their families were quickly shot to pieces. The rest surrendered, calling out for mercy and holding crying, terrified children in protective embrace.

The gunfire petered out to be replaced by the moans of the dying and wounded. Cattle lowed in distress and horses in harness nickered in panic. And over all rose the wailing of women confronted with the horror of the catastrophe that had fallen so suddenly and so brutally upon them and their loved ones. Around the stricken wagon train the outlaws rode watchful for signs of resistance.

'Get the valuables collected,' yelled McDonald as he holstered his six-shooter.

His men knew exactly what to do. 'Out, out,' they yelled at the survivors.

Traumatized, men, women and children were brutally hauled from the wagons if too slow to obey. Weapons were seized and tossed into the hillside. The outlaws were thorough in their searching.

Boxes and trunks were broken open and contents emptied on to the side of the trail. Whoops of delight accompanied valuable finds. Soon the ground was littered with clothes and precious documents as the bandits went through the wagons. Coins, jewellery and silverware were collected in bags taken from the wagons. When they had finished looting the bandits turned their attention to the survivors huddled miserably together. Five men and six women with a sprinkling of kids were all that remained. They watched apprehensively as one of the bandits approached.

'All your valuables,' he growled at them in a deep gravelly voice. He held out a gunnysack and waited. 'Now!' He suddenly — barked and fired a shot into the ground. There was a hurried scrambling to pull out wallets and watches and pathetic pieces of jewellery. 'Hurry, hurry,' growled the terrible man.

While this was going on their guide was cutting out horses from the wagons. The outlaws loaded the pack animals with their loot along with foodstuffs plundered from the wagons. At last they turned to the group of miserable travellers.

'Right — men one side — women over here.'

The outlaws gathered, smirking and relaxing somewhat now that the job was almost finished.

'We need women to cook, sew and bed us,' McDonald said, gazing at the small group of females. 'Any volunteers?'

This raised a howl of guffaws from

his men. Their eyes glittered greedily as they gazed with naked lust at the females. The women stirred uneasily and looked across at their menfolk for help. There was no help there. The men were as cowed as the women. McDonald raised his pistol and casually fired into the crowd of women. A small child was snatched back as the heavy slug punched her in the chest. The women screamed and scattered. A tall, dark-haired young woman knelt by the child's bleeding body.

'You brave man.' There were tears in her eyes as they blazed out at the killer. 'I only wish I had a gun. I'd do the same to you.'

McDonald smiled. 'You'll do, missy. You just volunteered to warm my bed tonight.'

The guide came forward leading a string of mounts. There was a mixture of mules and hacks.

'Climb aboard, girls. Paradise is a-coming.'

The women were forced to obey.

They were completely cowed — some weeping, some praying. They clambered awkwardly on to the mounts and clung there, miserable and lost. The men could only watch helplessly while their wealth and women were taken from them. There was worse to come.

At a nod from their leader the gang fanned out facing the survivors. The explosion of weapons was sudden and thunderous. The screams of the women mingled with the cries of the stricken men. Some men, only wounded during the first barrage, turned and tried to run for cover. Bullets quickly cut them down. One man was crawling towards the wagons, trailing blood from a stomach wound. Shots kicked up dust from his jacket and he ceased moving. As suddenly as it had started the shooting ended. Smoke curled up from the weapons of the gunmen. Women were shrieking hysterically. The smell of blood mingled with that of cordite.

Kid Conachy strode over to the women. 'Shut up! Shut up!' he screamed, pointing his gun to emphasize his order. The wailing tapered off, to be replaced by muffled sobbing.

'OK, move out,' McDonald called.

His men mounted their horses and the party got going. The noise of sobbing women subsided into the distance.

Those animals not killed in the raid and not needed by the raiders were left still harnessed to the wagons of their dead owners. They pulled unsuccessfully at the rigging, trying to break free. Their cries were mournful and pathetic.

A dark shape wheeled in the air above the scene of carnage. Another and another joined it. One by one they dropped out of the sky. They waddled to the dead bodies and began to feast.

3

Deputy Herbie Banner heard the horses stop outside the office. He cocked his head to one side and listened for a moment. The sound of horses stomping and blowing noisily went on but no one came to the door. Curiosity overcame his inertia and he jumped to his feet and went outside.

There were four horses at the hitching rail. No one had dismounted. On three of the mounts bodies were tied across the saddles. The fourth horse held a rider slumped forward as if weary beyond endurance.

'Jeez, is that you, Joe?'

The man straightened up and looked at Banner. A grunt emerged from a blood-encrusted face and then the deputy almost fell from his horse. Hastily Banner rushed to his colleague's aid.

'Drink,' croaked Hammer. 'I need a goddamn drink.'

'Jeez Joe, you need a doctor more'n a drink.'

'Just a crease, Herbie.' The voice slurred with tiredness. 'I'll be all right after a night's sleep, but first I need a drink.'

'What about these here bodies?' Banner stood and stared at the laden horses.

'Eh! Oh yeah. One of them's still alive. Get him in a cell, Herbie. I'll be over at McQueen's.'

Joe Hammer left his fellow deputy and walked away with a slightly unsteady gait. Banner stood scratching his head, staring after Hammer.

'Goddamn you, Joe — you sure are one cold-blooded, efficient bastard.'

Muttering his annoyance the deputy went through the bodies to find out which one was still alive.

Alf Deakin saw the man come in the saloon. He stared with some consternation. The face was a mask of dried blood. Even so, he thought there was something familiar about the man. Then he caught his breath. His hand reached for the bottle and glass. He walked the length of the bar and set the whiskey on the flap he used to enter and leave his workspace.

Hammer did not break stride till he was at the flap. Without a word to the barman he poured a stiff measure and swallowed with one quick swig. He poured a second measure and emptied it into the blood-encrusted lips.

Deakin stared with some concern at the deputy's face.

'Wanna talk about it?'

The flint-hard eyes stared back at him and the barman shivered. He had known Joe Hammer since he had come to Tiverton. Joe was a wild kid and, wanting excitement, had joined up as a deputy. Now after watching the lawman for four years' hunting of outlaws and killers, Alf Deakin had seen the kid grow into this cold-eyed manhunter.

'I guess not,' the barman muttered.

He began to wipe at a perfectly clean bar, slowly moving away from the formidable man now pouring himself a third drink.

Hammer was halfway down the bottle when Herbie Banner walked in and walked purposefully over to the bar.

'Goddamn it, Joe, I told you to go and see Doc Mason.' He ignored the cold-eyed stare directed at him. 'You look like hell.'

The sudden grin cracked some of the caked blood. 'I tell you something, Herbie.' The whiskey was starting to work and the big, golden-haired man was beginning to mellow. 'I sure feel like hell.'

Hammer felt someone nudge his arm. He tensed and his tortured body readied itself to lash out.

'Mister, you look troubled.'

Hammer looked at the female standing beside him. Long dark hair cascaded from a colourful ribbon tied around her head.

'Trouble, ma'am? I am trouble.' Hammer's voice was slurred as tiredness and whiskey took its toll on him.

The woman reached out a slim brown hand and took hold of his. To his own surprise and that of the watching men, Hammer let her.

'My spirit is telling me you are a true warrior destined for great things.'

By now Hammer's curiosity was aroused. He stared drunkenly at the strange female.

'I have drunk whiskey many times and slept with many women but never before have any ever tried to tell my fortune.'

'Have you the courage, Joe Hammer? Have you the courage to look into the future and see what fate has in store for you?'

The deputy threw back his head and laughed. It was a harsh sound in the midst of the sudden silence.

'I know my future. It is a plot of land on the outskirts of Tiverton measuring six feet by four. My name will be engraved on a stone. Deputy Joe Hammer — died of old age.' He laughed again.

The girl took his hand and lifting it from the bar turned it palm upwards. Fingers, strangely gentle and soothing, stroked his hand. It felt oddly comforting. The pain in his head eased slightly.

'I see a woman in your life. She waits for you. She awaits her warrior man. You will face great danger before you win her.'

Hammer was gawping at the woman. The hands were stroking the palm of his hand. A shiver passed through him. His eyes stared out from a blood-encrusted face and he could not move. He tried to laugh but could not bring the sound to the surface.

'There is a book. It is a holy book. I see you reading the book. But it is difficult to read. The letters in the book are covered in blood. Wait . . . wait a moment. The blood is clearing. I can read it now. The Hammer of God is written there.'

The woman took his hand and began leading him across the floor of the saloon. As if in a trance, a compliant Hammer went along with the strange female. She led him to the stairs. Hammer was unable to resist. He felt he should do something — call out, or laugh, or recover his hand, but instead he walked submissively upstairs with the young woman. She led him into one of the bedrooms.

4

Just before dusk the convoy pulled off the trail and headed into the hills. In a short time they came to a water hole. While the main body waited by the water, Pretty Boy and Black Charley dismounted and scouted the surrounding area. In a short time they returned and gave the all-clear.

'OK, folks,' McDonald called. 'Get some fires going and let's have some grub.'

Ordered about like slaves the wretched women set to work to serve the outlaws. In the gathering darkness and under the watchful eye of Growler they collected fuel for the fires. As night fell the smell of cooking filled the air.

While the food was being prepared the outlaws sat around making ribald remarks and swigging from bottles of whiskey. There were six women in the group. A few children had tagged along and sat in a miserable huddle. The buxom youngster who had spoken so bravely to McDonald was just seventeen. She was chubby and gangly with smouldering deep-set eyes.

'What's your name, Bright Eyes?' asked McDonald as she passed him a plate of beans and biscuits.

The young woman did not answer but threw him a hate-filled glance.

McDonald giggled. 'I can see I made a deep impression on you. Don't worry, first impressions can be all wrong. You'll grow to love me. That is if you last that long.'

As she turned to move away he grabbed the hem of her dress and dragged her down beside him.

'I likes a bit of company while I'm eating.'

The girl struggled to rise and McDonald punched her in the side of the head. She cried out and whirled on him, anger sparking in her face. He hit her again, this time on the mouth. She fell back and the gang leader sprawled on top of her.

In the morning some of the women were dead, as were the children. One of the women had somehow managed to find a knife and had almost severed her hands from her body. She was curled up in a congealing pool of blood. The bruised and bleeding survivors looked on her corpse with something akin to despair. But there was envy mixed in with their emotions. Her suffering was over; they still had to endure.

'Get the fires going, you lazy whores,' growled McDonald. He got to his feet and kicked the wretched women into action. The young woman favoured by the outlaw chief stumbled to her feet. Her face was a mass of bruises. As the bandits stirred from sleep the women got the fires lit and began the cooking process.

The smell of frying bacon and wood smoke mingled with the morning air. All around the camp the rustlers scratched at lice and vented wind. They struggled into boots and cussed the women for being too slow.

McDonald was standing and stamping his feet into his boots. He waved his hand towards the cook fire where the women were working. The men moved to the fire and McDonald ordered the women to serve out the food.

The young woman bitterly reflected on the world she had found. The wagon train had hired a guide to take them safely to their destination. That guide had betrayed them by leading their party to a bunch of vicious killers. Now she was forced to make coffee and cook breakfast for the brutes who had murdered her family and so cruelly abused her.

She wished now she had been killed along with her mother and father and brother. But thoughts of their murdered bodies lying back on the trail somehow gave her a fragment of resolution. While she still lived she might somehow find a way to hurt these vile beasts. She would survive and see these brutes punished.

Such wickedness could not go without retribution in a just world. A burst of laughter brought her to her senses.

McDonald was counting out banknotes. She watched with mounting bitterness as the guide moved up to receive his share. A deck of cards was produced, along with whiskey bottles.

Leah worked with the other wretched woman as they cleared up the breakfast things. Her hatred was growing like a live essence — worming inside and stiffening her resolve to stay alive.

'Get your asses over here.' The growling man was kicking at the women as he spoke. 'Boss says you gotta get rid of these bodies before they stink up the place.'

It was a harrowing experience. The women were weeping as they carried the bodies of the children from the camp. The young woman was pushed towards the suicide and fell on top of the corpse. She recoiled as her hands came in contact with the congealing blood. There was so much of it. She felt the bile rising and began to retch. Harsh laughter from behind hammered at her stretched nerves and she sobbed aloud. Her hand encountered the handle of the knife that had ended the poor woman's life. As she choked down her grief and rage the knife was slipped inside her dress.

5

Hammer turned and threw his arm across the bed. His hand flopped on to the mattress, finding nothing in the way. He groped for a moment, still finding nothing. At last he opened his eyes and raised his head. Grunting with the effort, he sat up. As he peered into the gloomy interior of the room he came to the inevitable conclusion he was alone. He relaxed back against the bolster. For long moments he lay motionless trying to recall the events of last night.

There had been the fight with the rustlers. Two dead, and one brought in live. He had no recollection of the shot that had toppled him from the saddle. Gently he probed the wound on his head. His fingers traced the scab that had formed along the crease. The pain had eased, though he still felt light-headed.

Through the hazy events of last night he recalled drinking at the bar. There had been pain and anger and exhaustion. He was drinking to forget how near he had come to death. Then the woman had accosted him. The broad picture was still vague but he was beginning to remember small details. She had led him upstairs and pushed him back on the bed.

'Let me ease your pain.'

Slim brown hands massaged and caressed his body. Somehow the discomfort and exhaustion had lessened. The pounding pain in his head had diminished. For the first time in his life someone else took control of his body.

Submerged in his mind there was a bad dream of faces of men he had killed. Faces from long back in his past, which he thought he had forgotten. His ruminations were interrupted by a knock on the door.

'Yeah!'

The door opened and the balding head of Herbie Banner appeared. He looked cautiously around the room before sliding inside.

Herbie was about forty, stockily built and a good man in a fight. He had a teenage son, Forrest, a bright youngster who wanted to become a deputy like his dad. This caused some friction between father and son, as Herbie wanted his son to go to law school.

'Sorry, Joe, I was worried you might still have company.' Hammer waited patiently. He knew Herbie wouldn't disturb him without reason.

'Bad news, Joe. McDonald struck again.'

Hammer sat up in the bed. 'God-damn it, where this time?'

'The old Fullers trail — it was a wagon train. We got a man down at the office as stumbled across them.'

Hammer was up now, pulling on his trousers. He was fastening his gunbelt as they left the room.

The oldster was slumped in his chair when the two deputies entered. He looked up and made as if to rise.

Banner waved him back.

'Tell it to Deputy Hammer just as you told me,' he instructed.

The old man rubbed a grimy hand across a weather-beaten face. He had taken his battered and stained hat from his head and this lay on his lap. As he talked he twisted and untwisted the frayed brim of the hat.

'I bin up in Gritty Mountain an' was comin' down fer supplies. Plumb run outta beans an' coffee.' He paused and rubbed his face again.

'You like a drink, old-timer?' Hammer moved to the cupboard on the wall as he spoke.

'Sure thing. When you boys finished with me I'm gonna git drunker than an Injun on moonshine.'

Hammer plonked three tin mugs on the desk and poured from a whiskey bottle.

'It war the smell. My ol' burro wouldn't go on. I had to git down and lead him forward. They was all lyin' there.' He shook his head and took a

41

swig of whiskey. 'Men, women and childer, weren't no one spared. Mister, I never seed anythin' like it afore. I hope I never live to see the like again.'

'How long you think they been there?'

'The way the buzzards had chewed them up I'd say no more'n a day.'

Hammer moved to the gun rack, took down a rifle and laid it on the desk. He began to fill his jacket pockets with cartridges.

'Joe, what the hell are you doing?'

Hammer turned and looked at Banner. His eyes were bleak.

'What do you think? I'm going after them.'

'Joe, hang on, now. You know we can't ride out without the say-so from Judge Cordway. If he comes back and finds you gone he'll rip you a month's pay.'

Hammer turned a bleak face to his friend. 'You tell Judge Cordway to stick his say-so up his ass. If I wait for him, them killers will be long gone. They

42

getting cocky now. Never hit this close afore. I have a chance while the trail is still fresh to track them.' He turned to the door. 'You keep the office warm till I get back, Herbie.'

'Goddamn you to hell an' back, Joe Hammer.' Grabbing his own weapons, Banner ran after his companion. 'I ain't letting you go out there alone. Might as well we both face the wrath of Cordway.'

6

Not knowing how long they would be out on the trail, in order to conserve their horses the deputies kept them down to a steady pace. Before they left Tiverton they had thrown together supplies of coffee, beans and biscuits. At first they rode in grim silence, the old prospector's description of the slaughter haunting their thoughts. The day was still young and showed promise of another spell of fiercely hot sunshine.

'Joe, I been thinking about you and that woman last night.'

'What about it?' Hammer did not turn his head.

'She said some mighty odd things.' When there was no response from his companion Herbie ploughed on. 'She said about that blood book that would rule your life. What did she mean by that?'

44

'Hell I know, Herbie. This fortune telling is all guess-work. The only book I read is the Bible. She got that part right anyway. Most people read the Bible so she was safe guessing I would be the same. The blood bit is easy too. I'm a deputy. How many deputies you know ain't killed someone at some stage in their career? It just so happens I kill a few more than your average lawman.

'So, I read the Bible. I try to live by the code of the Bible. Occasionally I havta kill during my job. That's where the blood comes in. Then she called me the Hammer of God. Put all those things together and you got a fortune laid out. How difficult is that? Now let's change the subject. How is that son of yours getting along?'

'Son of a bitch, wants to become a deputy. I want him to take more schooling. That way he just might do better for himself. Joe, would you talk to Forrest? Try and talk him out of joining. He sure looks up to you. He thinks you're some kinda hero.'

His companion laughed out loud. 'You sure Forrest is as bright as you say he is? Hero! I'm a goddamn deputy. I hunt down the scum that make this country unsafe for decent folks that want to make a good life. That don't make me no hero. Sometimes I think I'm no different from the men as I go after.'

'Joe, you know that ain't true. You're a good lawman. There's no one I'd rather have at my back than Joe Hammer in a tight spot.'

This time Hammer did turn round and stare earnestly at his companion. 'Herbie, you been drinking afore we set out?'

Herbie grinned mischievously. 'Nope. The way I figure it, I got to keep in with the Hammer of God. When I get to heaven you might just be promoted to gateman. I just wanna hedge my bets and when I get to the gates of heaven that gateman won't forget old comrades.'

'Banner, if I hear any more of that nonsense about me being the Hammer of God I'm gonna get off this horse and beat the living daylights out of you.'

'OK, OK, keep your goddamn hair on, Joe. Can't you take a joke?'

After that they rode in silence, each sunk in their own thoughts.

As the old prospector had said, it was the smell that alerted the horses and made them skittish. Even so the deputies were not prepared for the horrific scene of death.

'Jesus, Joe, is there a God in heaven at all, to allow this to happen?

They dismounted, tied up their mounts and manoeuvred through the plundered wagons. Even with bandannas pressed against the face the smell was unbearable. Scavengers had worried at the carcasses. The sight of the partly dismembered children's bodies was particularly heartrending.

Hammer crouched to examine a spoil of spent cartridges and the group of dead bodies nearby.

'They lined the men up and shot them down,' he observed. Casting round he found the clutter of hoof-prints.

'Looks like they loaded up here. Must have taken some of the women with them. God help them.'

He moved up the track looking for signs of the departure.

'Bring up the horses, Herbie. We'll track them from here.'

They rode along, following the tracks. After a while Herbie broke the silence between them.

'No one has ever survived their raids before. Those poor women are in for a hellish time with them devils.'

'No survivors — no witnesses,' Hammer answered. He turned bleak eyes on Banner. 'For our sake, I just hope they stop along the way to dally with those poor women folk.'

'Goddamn it, Joe! That's a helluva thing to say!'

His companion did not answer. And for a while they concentrated on following the outlaws' tracks. It was nudging towards noon when Hammer signalled a halt.

'Herbie, looks like we lost the trail. They musta turned off somewhere. Goddamn it, we'll have to split up and cast around both sides of the line. If we find anything we'll havta risk a shot. Just one gunshot and hope it don't spook them. About an hour before sundown we'll meet up.' Hammer cast round for a landmark. 'Over there by that big bunch of cottonwoods. We'll camp up there for the night and start out again in the morning.'

'OK, Joe, I can't get those poor women out of my mind.' Herbie spurred off to one side of the track. 'Good luck,' he called over his shoulder.

'Good luck!' muttered Joe Hammer.

When the shot came it brought Hammer up short. He felt a grim satisfaction as he wheeled his mount around and headed towards the sound. Minutes later he saw someone waving a hat in the air to attract his attention.

With some relief he saw it was Banner. Herbie was afoot and holding his horse's reins in his hand.

'What you got, Herbie?'

'I reckon I found the tracks of them there bandits.' Banner turned and pointed. 'I scouted all the way past that rise over there. Looks like a large party passed this way.'

'Well done, Herbie. We'll go and take a look.'

They both dismounted at the point Banner indicated and cast round for tracks. Hammer pushed back his hat and scratched his golden head.

'Seems to me you're right. If they stay on that direction it takes them towards them foothills.'

He raised a hand and pointed towards a dark line on the horizon. The deputy stared off into the distance, his brow furrowed in thought.

'Herbie, I wanna follow that bunch into those foothills if you're willing. There's a lot of pony tracks. There could be up to a dozen in the gang. You up for it, or do you wanna head back to Tiverton for reinforcements? But I gotta hunch by the time we do all that they'll be long gone.'

'Joe, I seen you and your hunches afore. I'll hang on in there. You might just need someone to cover your ass.'

Joe Hammer grinned bleakly. 'Let's go, pardner. I just hope I'm right and we catch up with them murdering varmints.'

7

Deputy Joe Hammer cradled his rifle against his shoulder and traversed the sights around the encampment. He was trying to decide which of the bandits would be most dangerous. From wanted posters he had a good idea who was in the camp. With his flamboyant style of dress Pretty Boy Johnstone was easily recognizable. So far he had identified McDonald and two big men he assumed were Gratten and Patterson. It nagged Hammer that the whole gang was not in camp. The only other occupants of the encampment were a couple of ragged women crouching by a cook fire. He had to assume the other members of the gang were on a mission of some sort.

They had found the outlaw camp more by accident than skilful tracking. Hammer had sent Banner round to the opposite side. Now he waited patiently for his partner to get into position. Banner was to yell out a warning to the bandits to surrender. Assuming the warning would be ignored, Hammer had to decide which of the bandits to take out first.

McDonald would be the most formidable member. The fact that he was lounging against a tree and was partly obscured by a heap of saddles made him a difficult target. The deputy decided to change position in order to get a clearer shot at the bandit leader. Before he could do so he paused as a man stumbled into the camp. There was something familiar about the figure. Another man appeared behind the newcomer and prodded him with a revolver.

'Goddamn it to hell,' Hammer cursed as he recognized Herbie.

The other outlaws were turning towards the two men. McDonald climbed to his feet and walked across to them. Hammer guessed the man who had apprehended Banner was Kid Conachy. He reckoned that accounted for all the gang. In that he was mistaken.

'Just take your finger of that there trigger.' The voice came from somewhere behind the deputy. 'Any sudden move and I'll take out your spine.'

Hammer went very still.

'Leave the rifle there and roll away from it. I want you lying face down.'

There was nothing for it but to obey. As he rolled he saw the dark shape of the black man — the .45 in his big fist looking like a toy. In accounting for the outlaws he had missed out Black Charley Jordan. Hammer felt his gun being removed from the holster.

'OK, mister, you stand up real careful and walk down there to join your friend.'

As Hammer rose and walked towards the camp he saw McDonald lash out with his pistol and catch Herbie Banner across the face with the barrel. The deputy staggered back and the Kid

Conachy drove his rifle butt into his back. Herbie went down with a groan.

'Well, what have we here?' McDonald snarled as he saw Hammer. 'Are we in the midst of a deputy convention?'

As Hammer came within range the outlaw chief lashed out at him with his pistol, catching the deputy on the side of the head. The heavy gun connected with the barely healed wound and with a grunt Hammer went down on his knees opposite his partner.

The pain was agonizing and blood poured in a stream down the side of the deputy's face. Before he could recover a boot hit him in the chest and drove him on to his back. The same boot was suddenly in his throat and McDonald was staring down at him, aiming his pistol into the deputy's face.

'I want some answers,' he snarled. 'What are you two doing out here and how come you found us?'

'Trailed you from the wagon train,' Hammer croaked.

'Goddamn liar!'

The boot pressed harder while McDonald spoke to his men.

'You two get back out there. See if there's any more lawmen lurking on our tail.'

Keeping his boot firmly in his throat the outlaw chief turned his attention back to the deputy.

'We covered our tracks pretty good. Someone led you to us?'

'No one . . . was tracking you . . . '

Lacking oxygen as the boot pressed even harder, and groggy from the bang on his head, Hammer passed out.

When he came to someone was bending over him. He squinted through part-opened eyes. Then he opened wide. He could make out a young woman crouched by him, dabbing at the blood on his face. Her face was almost as bruised as his Blood leaking from her nose and mouth had smeared dark stains across her face.

Seeing he was awake she put her finger to her lips and then carefully put her hand inside her torn dress.

Hammer was puzzled by her behaviour till he saw the large knife she produced. With a covert movement she slipped the blade inside his jacket.

'I'll get you some food,' she said. 'Are you hungry?'

She jerked suddenly as a fist smacked her on the side of the head.

'Who told you to mess with the prisoners?' A savage kick accompanied the question.

Looming over them was the bandit Hammer guessed to be Jesse Patterson — a big man with muscular shoulders. The outlaw's attention was all on the girl as she scrambled on all fours to get away from him. Hammer came up with the knife in his hand. He drove it hard up into the outlaw's belly angling it towards the heart.

Not knowing whether he was observed Hammer clamped his free hand over the big man's gaping mouth, all the while twisting and turning the blade inside the struggling man's rib cavity. They went down with Hammer on top.

He gripped the holstered pistol and rolled away from the violently twitching body as the man haemorrhaged his life's blood into the dirt.

Amazingly none of the other bandits had noticed the scuffle. The outlaw leader, McDonald, was back at his seat by the tree. Growler and Pretty Boy were playing a desultory game of cards.

Herbie Banner was starting to his feet, his eyes on his partner. Patterson had ceased moving. Holding the purloined pistol at the ready Hammer jerked the blood-stained knife from the body of the big bandit. He threw the knife to Herbie.

'More whiskey, Bright Eyes,' McDonald suddenly roared out.

As she moved to obey, his eyes took in the scene. He did not immediately react. Hammer fired and the outlaw chief jerked back as the deputy's slug hit him in the shoulder. With quick reactions he rolled behind the stack of saddles.

Hammer ran towards the card-players. He snapped off two shots and was close enough not to miss. Pretty Boy was hit in the ear and the bullet took out the left side of his head. He keeled over hardly knowing what had hit him. Growler was unfortunate to be hit in the throat. He fell back clutching his neck as blood pumped in bright streams through his clutching fingers.

A shot whined past him as McDonald tried to shoot at the running deputy. Hammer threw himself beside the fallen card-players, rolling behind them to keep the bodies between himself and the man shooting at him. Growler was twisting and making gurgling noises as he tried to hold in his life with blood-discoloured fingers. Hammer ignored him and quickly frisked the downed bandits for weapons.

Pretty Boy Johnstone had twin fancy pistols. The deputy pulled both weapons and, risking a bullet from McDonald, he rose high enough to throw one of them as hard as he could towards Banner. Not waiting to see if Herbie got the weapon he dropped flat as bullets flew past his head. Some were thudding into the bodies the deputy was sheltering behind. Growler ceased moving as the bullets from the outlaw boss's gun hit home.

Hammer fired towards the pile of saddles but could see no clear target. He knew this had to be ended quickly, before the other bandits returned.

Herbie had retrieved Pretty Boy's pistol and fired a shot at McDonald. Hammer began snaking sideways in an attempt to circle round the bandit chief. Herbie saw his manoeuvre and fired again to give him cover. Hammer caught a glimpse of someone stirring within the camp. The young girl who had passed him the knife was stepping back from the campfire, a pot gripped in both hands. Steam was leaking from the pan.

'Goddamn woman,' he muttered, shaking his head and then wishing he hadn't, as pain throbbed through his temples. 'She's worried about the stew while our lives are on the line.'

Herbie fired again and drew answering shots from the outlaw. The girl was circling behind the pile of saddles sheltering the outlaw chief.

'Bloody woman, if he spots her he'll shoot her.'

His mouth gaped open as the woman swung the pot. The steaming brew sailed out and doused the man sheltering in the pile of saddles. Hammer was already running forward, the hand with the pistol held out in front of him but holding his fire while he waited to get a clear shot.

The head and shoulders of a bellowing McDonald rose into sight. Steam was erupting from his head and face. He was yelling and swinging round with his gun and sighting on the young woman. Hammer fired and kept on firing. McDonald got a couple of shots off before the deputy's bullets struck home and the outlaw's head disappeared.

Hammer threw himself over the pile of saddles. He landed on the prone body of the outlaw chief.

'Jesus!' he exclaimed as his hand bore down on the carcass. His fingers sank into one of the wounds he had blasted into the outlaw chief.

By the saddles were Hammer's own weapons. Quickly he retrieved them, all the time watching for the return of the big black man and Kid Conachy. The young woman was sitting on the grass with the empty pan by her side. Steam was still rising from the pot. As he glanced at her Hammer saw the dark figure standing about a dozen yards beyond her.

Black Charley Jordan was surveying the camp in some bewilderment, taking in the sprawled bodies left in the deputy's wake. The movement by the pile of saddles drew his attention. His gun was coming round. Hammer was bringing his own gun up, McDonald's blood on his hands making the weapon slippery. He tensed as he waited for the expected bullet while he tried to get a proper grip on the Colt. Then the young woman sitting on the ground screamed. She was holding out blood-stained hands and looking down at the blood oozing from the hole in her chest. The scream was a high-pitched and unnerving sound — startling in its intensity.

The black man started and glanced towards the girl. It was enough. Hammer steadied the Colt. He loosed off two close-spaced shots. They took the black man in the chest. He staggered back, his eyes opening wide — showing startlingly white in the dark visage. The nozzle of his weapon was dipping and then his knees buckled and he went down.

Knowing there was another armed bandit still unaccounted for Hammer did not relax. He clambered to his feet, sweeping his gun around the perimeter of the camp. A flurry of shots drew his attention to the far side where Banner was holed up. He was just in time to see a man stagger into sight. In his hand he was clutching a revolver.

Hammer lined up his own weapon but held his fire as he saw the man was having difficulty standing upright. He saw Banner to the left of the man covering him with his still smoking weapon. The bandit pitched forward on to his face and lay still.

Slowly, but slowly, silence settled on the scene. Hammer could hear a woman weeping. He realized another woman had been cowering on the ground while all the action had been going on. Wearily he sagged back and sat on the saddles. He stared across at the young woman who had saved his skin. She was lying on the ground. Her eyes were wide open and staring sightlessly. Hammer imagined there was accusation in those blank eyes as if she was blaming him for failing to keep her alive.

8

The little caravan dawdled along — the riders tiredly drooping in the saddles. Herbie Banner headed the procession. A lead rope trailed from his pommel guiding a file of horses carrying the remains of the dead outlaws and their victims. A weary looking fair-haired woman in her late thirties rode behind the dead bodies. To the rear of the column rode Deputy Joe Hammer.

The lawmen, along with the surviving female, had decided to start back for Tiverton straightaway. No one wanted to linger at the camp that held so many terrible memories.

There was little or no conversation among the riders. Bone-weary and sore in mind and body they rode with the glazed expression of shocked survivors still coming to terms with the realization that they had survived.

As night drew in the travellers could see the lights of Tiverton in the distance. The illuminations glowed like welcoming beacons in the twilight. The horses, sensing home, picked up the pace. The woman guided her mount alongside Hammer.

'What will happen when we get to Tiverton?' she asked.

'I guess we'll find you temporary accommodation with Doc Mason and his wife. You can stay there till we contact your folks.'

'My folks,' she said dully, 'are back there with that wagon train.'

They rode in silence for a moment.

'I'm just glad they're all dead. I . . . I mean those brutes. Is that wicked of me to be glad?'

'There was once a much-tried man called Job. I can only quote you a verse from his story. It might just make things a mite clearer. *Thou knowest that I am not wicked; and there is none that can deliver me out of thine hand.*'

'Thank you, Deputy. There is some

comfort in your words.'

After that they rode in silence.

Doc Mason and his wife Cynthia were a warm and reassuring couple. They immediately took charge of the weary refugee.

'A bath and a hot meal will work wonders,' Cynthia Mason asserted.

She was a plump, matronly woman with a round, kind face. One felt instinctively that she would gather you to her bosom and keep at bay the nasty things of the world. As the only survivor of the wagon train was hustled away into the bowels of the house the doctor eyed Joe Hammer.

'Joe, you come on in here and let me look at that head.'

'It's all right, Doc. I need a drink more than you looking at my head.'

For answer, Doc Mason took the deputy's arm and led him inside the house.

'There's probably nothing inside that thick skull of yours, only sawdust, but I'd like to take a look anyway.'

'Doc, I gotta look after the horses and report back to Judge Cordway.'

Joe Hammer looked over his shoulder to see his partner gazing wearily after him.

'Don't worry, Joe. I'll take care of the horses and do any reporting.'

Still protesting, Hammer was led inside the doctor's house.

Herbie Banner mounted again and surveyed the horse herd he was supposed to care for. As he was wondering how he was going to manage he heard a voice calling. Racing down the dirt street towards him was Herbie's son.

'Gosh, Pa, I'm glad to see you're back.' Forrest suddenly caught sight of the horses with their gruesome burdens. He stopped abruptly. 'Pa, is that the McDonald gang?'

'Sure is, son. That's the outlaw's pay-off. He either comes into town draped over a horse or ends up dancing on the end of a rope. Not much of a recommendation for a life of banditry.

You're just in time to help me with these horses. You jump on board one of these nags and we'll head over to the jail.'

'Sure, Pa.' Forrest clambered on to a saddle and grabbed a lead rope. He glanced round anxiously at his father. 'Where's Hammer? He ain't dead, is he?'

'Hammer, nah. Take more than a bunch of low-grade outlaws to finish Joe Hammer. He's had a knock on the head. Doc Mason's patching him up just now. While he's lying on Doc's couch being pampered your old dad gets to do all the dirty work.'

'Do I get deputy's pay for this, Pa?' Forrest was obviously enjoying the role of helper.

'You'll get put across my knee and spanked if you give me any more lip, you young scallywag.'

'Gee Pa, I guess I'm too old for you to paddle.'

'Don't you believe it, son. We just whupped the McDonald gang. You think a little whippersnapper like you can defy the great Banner — lawman extraordinary?'

'Pa, I just know you didn't do it without help from Joe Hammer. And if you try to spank me I'll tell Hammer. Anyway, when I next see Judge Cordway I'm gonna ask him for a start. I reckon I'm old enough to train for a deputy's badge.'

'Goddamn it, Forrest, I told you to stay at the schooling. You'll do more good as a lawyer than you'll ever do as a badge-toting lawman.'

Father and son were still arguing when they pulled up at the jailhouse on the main drag. There was a light on inside. Banner dismounted wearily and turned to his son.

'Keep an eye on things till I report to the judge.' He pushed inside and was surprised to see that the occupant wasn't his chief. 'Marshal Dunkley, what the hell are you doing here?'

Charlie Dunkley, a big, heavily muscled young man with a round, open face, grinned up at Banner.

'Herbie, you look like hell. What in tarnation you been up to?'

'Just brung in the McDonald gang. Thought Judge Cordway was here.'

Dunkley was up from his seat instantly and coming round the desk.

'Goddamnit — the McDonald gang! You're one ring-tailed bobcat, Herbie. That's why I'm here. Senator Custer sent for me to find out if you needed help to bring in that bunch.'

He grabbed Banner's hand and began pumping it enthusiastically.

'Hang on, Charlie. I had some help. Hammer put most of them away. I just loaded the bodies.'

'Bodies! I might have known if Hammer was involved. Does he ever bring in anyone alive?'

'Christ, Charlie, Hammer is the best lawman we have. He's cleaned up this territory almost single handed.'

Before the lawmen could continue the door burst open and an older man entered. His face was suffused with anger.

'What the hell's going on here?' He glared belligerently at Herbie Banner. 'Banner, is that your mess outside? And what the hell's the idea leaving a kid in charge? This is a law office not a schoolroom.'

'Judge Cordway, we just brought in the McDonald gang. That's them outside draped over them there horses.'

'You brung them in dead!' The judge's face was red with either drink or anger or both. 'We need witnesses! We need prisoners to testify! We need criminals to be tried in court! When were you appointed judge to pronounce the death sentence?'

The two lawmen stared in bemusement at the judge.

'And where is Hammer? Just tell me he is one of the bodies out there.'

'No . . . no, he's down at the doc's getting patched up.'

'So we got no witnesses! No one to tell us what happened out there. Only Hammer and you to make up whatever story suits your own purposes.'

'Evening, Judge.'

No one had noticed the door open until Hammer spoke. The deputy, a white bandage visible under his black hat, stood in the doorway staring bleakly at the men inside.

'Hammer. What the hell's the meaning of this? Can't you bring anyone in alive?'

Flinty eyes stared back at the older man.

'I'm off duty, Judge Cordway. If you want me. I'll be down at McQueen's. I need a drink to take the bad taste out of my mouth.'

Before anyone could react Hammer turned on his heel and left. The street door slammed loudly behind him.

'You were wrong, Judge, about witnesses.' Some of the coldness that Hammer had shown had now transferred to Banner. 'We brung in a woman. She is the sole survivor of the ambushed wagon train. Doc Mason's looking after her. You want to know what happened, ask her. And then ask her if she thought justice was served.'

9

Joe Hammer's eyes snapped open. He stared wildly round the room as he tried to still his fast-beating heart. His hand hit something smooth and round in the bed beside him. He picked up the empty whiskey bottle and flung it against the wall. There was a satisfying crash as it hit and broken glass cascaded to the floor.

All night he had wrestled with his demons. A parade of dead men had marched in an endless line through his dreams. They were men he had killed during his term as lawman. The dead men pointed to the dreadful wounds on their bodies. Most terrible was the knowledge that he could not remember the names of this army of slain. But they were determined he should not forget.

'Thomas Peterson,' a balding man in

a bloodstained nightshirt announced. 'You caught me in bed with that whore. I shudda killed you.'

'John Thrasher.' Part of the ghost's head was missing. 'That rifle shell took out most of my brain. I had you in my sights. I wish I'd been faster on the trigger.'

Andy Weathers, Henry Matheson, Stewart Shirley, Tod Thompson . . . the parade of the dead seemed to go on all night, their ghastly wounds dripping gore and leaving a trail of blood across the bedroom.

He woke up screaming when the young woman who had helped him at the outlaw's camp lurched past. She said nothing. Her bloody and torn clothes said it all. The black holes of her eyes stared out at him while tears of blood dribbled down her face.

For a long time he lay as he was, afraid to close his eyes in case he fell asleep, and once again found himself at the mercy of his ghouls. At last his heart stopped pounding and his breathing returned to normal. Slowly he sat up in the sweat-soaked bed. There was a bad taste in his mouth. His eyes felt hot and dry. The bedclothes were twisted about his body where he had tossed and turned as he wrestled with his demons. He rubbed at his face and felt the stubble of several days' growth.

'How long have I been out?' he wondered.

Slowly memory came back. There had been the fight at the camp of the outlaw McDonald. He remembered the intense sadness he had felt at the death of the young woman who had slipped him the knife. Everything else was lost in a grey fog. He knew he had been drinking. He did not need the empty bottle in his bed to remind him. But forgetfulness could not be found in a bottle. If anything it only enhanced the demons that of late had haunted him.

'How many have I killed?' he whispered.

The appalling thing was that he had no idea. After the first few killings he had lost count of the dead outlaws he had to his tally. The drinking sessions after each episode helped at the beginning. Now it was obvious the alcohol was no longer blotting out the voices of his victims.

He held a hand up before his face. His fingers had a pronounced tremor. Slowly he edged to the side of the bed and lowered his feet to the floor. After a few attempts he managed to stand upright. Gritting his teeth against the nausea that swept over him he lurched to the window. He swept back the curtains. Daylight flooded into the room temporatily blinding him. He squeezed his eyes shut.

'Goddamn it, Joe Hammer, what the hell are you doing to yourself?' he muttered. 'Twenty-four years of age and you've lost count of the men you've killed.'

He tried to shake the morbid thoughts loose but they refused to be driven away. The memory of his nightmares kept trying to resurface. At last he turned and began to gather his clothes. Slowly he struggled to get dressed. For a long time he stared at the gunbelt with the lethal Army Colt nestling in the holster, wondering whether he should leave it behind in the hotel. In the end he belted the rig in place. When he stood the familiar weight of the weapon made him realize how much it was part of his life.

He trudged downstairs. He had a permanent room at McQueen's saloon. As he came downstairs he walked straight towards the exit. He heard Alf Deakin calling out a greeting and waved his hand in acknowledgement without turning around.

'Shave and bath,' he growled as he stepped inside Leverett Spring's barbershop.

There was one other customer in the chair.

'Sure thing, Mr Hammer. Be with you presently.'

It was while he soaked in the bath he made up his mind.

'Goddamn it, I've had enough,' he growled out loud.

Chase, the half-wit employed by Leverett Spring to wait on the needs of the bathers, looked up.

'You got five minutes left, Mr Deputy Sheriff,' he said as he reached for the towel.

'Chase, you ever killed anyone?'

'I don't think so Mr Deputy Sheriff,' Chase replied after pondering this for a time. 'I just do the baths and run errands.'

Hammer studied the vacant-looking face for a moment.

'You know, in a way I envy you, Chase. Does anything ever bother you? Like do you have bad dreams or anything?'

Chase dropped his gaze and a flush started in his neck, spreading up into his vacuous face.

'You gonna put me in jail, Mr Deputy Sheriff? I never meant no harm.'

'What the hell you talking about?'

The youth was sinking lower and lower into his chair, the flush deepening.

'I just look, honest, Mr Deputy Sheriff The females don't know I watch.' He squirmed uncomfortably in his seat. 'Then I have the bad dreams. Don't put me in jail. I promise I won't do it no more.'

'Gimme the goddamn towel,' Joe growled as understanding came. 'Jesus, there was me beginning to envy you thinking your life must be pretty damn uncomplicated.'

He stood up in the washtub and snatched the towel from the frightened man.

Judge Cordway had a set of offices five or six stores away from the jail. When Joe Hammer strode inside and asked to see the judge he was kept waiting for ten minutes. It did not bother him. The judge always kept people waiting. Joe was used to it. So he sat patiently on an uncomfortable wooden chair and waited.

'Well, so the mighty Joe Hammer deigns to turn up for work.'

For the first time the young deputy noticed how old the judge looked. His face was lightly creased and puffy. Dark pouches hung beneath his eyes, giving him a slightly benign look. Joe was not fooled. Judge Cordway was a hard and ruthless man. He used his deputies like slaves, driving them and badgering them into doing more than their stint of duty demanded.

'I got a job for you, Hammer.' The judge was reaching for documents on his desk. 'I want you to collect a prisoner from Dimitry. They're holding him for murder and arson and want to send him over here for trial. Shouldn't take you more'n a couple of days.' He had the documents in his hand as he looked up at his deputy. 'Nice straight-forward job for you after the easy week you've just had.' The older man put a sneer into his voice as he spoke the last sentence.

Slowly Joe Hammer reached up and

unpinned his badge.

'Sorry, Cordway.' He deliberately left off the judge's title. 'You'll havta get yourself another screwed-up zombie to do your dirty work.' He tossed the badge on the table. 'I resign.'

'Joe, you can't do this. You — '

Whatever else he said was cut of by the slamming of the door.

PART TWO

THE HAMMER
RE-FORGED

*Is not my word as like a fire? saith the
Lord; and like a hammer that breaketh
the rock in pieces.*

Jeremiah 50:23

10

The old priest, thinking he was unobserved, stood watching the monk working in the garden. The novice was wearing the brown robes of the Order of St Francis. His golden hair hung down, obscuring his features.

'You checking up on my gardening methods, Father Nostrill?'

The old priest laughed. 'Brother Joseph, you never fail to amaze me. No matter from what direction I approach you always know I am there. I used to believe living in a monastery gave me softness in my walk. No matter how quiet I step you are never taken by surprise.'

'Guilty conscience, I suppose on my part. I don't want to be caught idling when I'm supposed to be working.'

'That I do not believe, Brother Joseph. If anyone in this monastery works hard it is you.'

Brother Joseph stood. He was tall and his broad shoulders stretched the rough woollen habit that was the garb of the brothers living and working in the monastery.

'Certainly if your garden produce is an indication of how hard you work it speaks volumes for your efforts. We've never had such largesse from our vegetable patch.'

The young monk smiled slightly at this praise from his superior.

'Come and see me after matins this evening,' Father Nostrill requested of the monk. 'I have something important to discuss with you.'

The priest did not miss the flicker of unease that showed for a second in the young monk's eyes. He smiled to himself as he turned away to continue his walk. Brother Joseph stood staring after the old priest before turning back to his vegetable garden.

The ancient melodies of plainchant drifted up from the chapel as the monks praised their God. Brother Joseph stood head and shoulders above his brethren. He was easily the biggest man in the congregation and also the youngest. His hymn book was grasped in strong, work-hardened fingers. As he sang with his brothers he cast occasional glances at the priest officiating at the ceremony. Father Nostrill was unaware of these surreptitious looks he was receiving. He stood before the congregation, shoulders bowed with age, his eyes closed in contemplation.

Evensong ended and the monks dispersed. Some of the more devout stayed at their benches to pray and meditate while others chose to do so in the privacy of their cells. Brother Joseph rose and walked through the corridors of the monastery till he reached his superior's room. He knocked timidly on the door of the study.

'Come,' the voice invited him.

The old priest was seated at his window looking out at the darkening sky.

'You know that tonight, Brother, there will be an eclipse of the moon?' he asked.

'I did not, Father.'

'Come, we will observe together from my window.'

Brother Joseph joined his superior and they sat with their knees almost touching by the window.

'See how the shadow is nibbling away at the round shape of our moon.'

'Indeed Father, it makes one feel very humble to see this.'

'That is how I imagine our lives to be measured. We arrive in this vale of tears with the light of God shining within us. A dark shadow encroaches on our lives as we grow to maturity. Only when we embrace the light of our Lord again will the shadow pass.'

Both men sat silent gazing up as the eclipse progressed.

'Brother Joseph, it is exactly six months since you rode up to our humble monastery and asked to be taken in. My thoughts, when I first laid eyes on you were that you were an outlaw on the run and needed a hideout. You had the look of a man fleeing from something. Let's face it, where better to hide from the law than a monastery. You even had the weapons of your trade with you. When I told you that you could stay for as long as you wished you removed those weapons and handed them to me. I remember you telling me to sell them and to use the money to feed the poor.'

The old man rose and walked to a large wooden chest. Opening the lid he extracted a cloth-wrapped bundle. He carried this across and set it on the windowsill.

'To my shame I never did what you asked. I feared the violence I could detect within you. I sensed that someday you would come seeking these instruments of death.'

The priest put out a hand and rested it on the cloth. Brother Joseph stared at the hand. It looked old and frail, the skin almost translucent.

'You are not content here, Brother Joseph. I sense a wildness in you — a restless spirit that will never be at peace. You pace the corridors of this monastery like a caged animal needing to be free but fearing the big bad world out there.' The hand lifted and a finger pointed to the sky. 'See, Brother, how the moon is in shadow now. Note the red glow that has emerged. That, Brother is how this world in which we live really is. The dark shadow of sin creeps across our world. Then the violence begins and everything is drenched in blood.'

Both men sat staring out at the dark red glow that obscured the moon.

'Brother Joseph, I am pleased to say that I was wrong about you.'

For the first time the monk looked directly at the priest.

'Wrong?'

He watched as a smile spread on that gentle old face. The priest had a broad head with thinning grey hair brushed straight back. His face, like his hands, was almost transparent and, in spite of his age, unlined.

'You have lived here this past half year in an exemplary manner, as befits a man of God. I believe whatever life you lived before coming to San Christobel has been washed from your soul by your diligence and holy behaviour. Not only have you applied yourself to the cleansing of your past but you have also been most diligent in learning Spanish. In view of this I want you to partake more fully in the life of our community.

'As you know, Father Sebastian teaches the village children. The good father is, like myself, getting old and feeble. He will not admit it for he dearly loves his classes. I notice you are most able in your writing and reading skills. Tomorrow I want you to accompany Father Sebastian to the village and help him with his tasks of teaching. However,' a smile was playing round the priest's mouth, 'do not let him think you are helping but the other way round. He is teaching you.'

'Thank you, Father. It is an honour I do not deserve.'

'One more thing, Brother Joseph, before you retire for the night. Think about taking your vows. I believe you are ready for that next step in your redemption.'

11

It was early in the day. The sky was a smooth cobalt-blue with a blistering sun pouring out a parching heat that bled every drop of moisture from man and beast. Nothing much moved in the little hamlet of San Christobel. Father Sebastian sat at the rear of the adobe church with a bevy of small children, some just infants in arms. A separate group of boys and girls, slightly older, sat with Brother Joseph.

The large roomy church dominated the village. Because of the thickness of the walls the church was the coolest place in the village. The steps of the church led down to a spacious plaza bordered with various adobe structures.

Brother Joseph was reading from a large Bible. The children sat about with varying degrees of inattention. Pepe and Geraldo had two racing beetles and the contest between their pets kept them totally absorbed. Juan was dozing. Maria and Dolores were discussing the merits of the handsome padre with the golden hair.

'That scar on his head he got in a duel over a beautiful woman.' Dolores sighed. 'The man he fought the duel with wounded him on his head with a sabre. Then Brother Joseph killed him and he had to flee the *rurales*. The beautiful woman they fought over died of heartbreak.'

'No, he was a soldier. He was in love with the general's daughter. The general caught them together and shot him with his pistol, wounding his head. Then he had him drummed out of the army. He has come here to forget her. She was very beautiful.'

Brother Joseph observed all this inattention. He was supposed to read passages to the children which had been specially chosen to enhance their Christian duties. Mostly they were taken from the New Testament: the

Sermon on the Mount, readings from St Paul. He glanced over at Father Sebastian. The old priest was absorbed in the task of teaching his young charges.

'How would you feel if your brothers were killed when they were born?' Brother Joseph suddenly asked. 'Dolores, how many brothers have you in your family?'

The young girl looked faintly surprised. 'I have five brothers, Brother Joseph.' And she named them for him.

'Just imagine there was a law that all male children were killed as soon as they were born.'

'That's just cruel. There would be no law like that ever passed.'

'Right, just imagine you were living in Texas and the United States of America passed a law to kill or imprison every male who was not a white American.'

Slowly their interest was being stirred. A lively debate started. Even the racing beetles were forgotten as their owners became involved.

'Well that's just what happened at the time Moses was born. He should have been put to death but his mother wrapped him up nice and snug in a blanket and put him in a little basket. She then pushed him out into the river Nile in his little basket boat. Can anyone tell me what happened after that?'

They were hooked. Their interest quickened as they discussed good and bad laws and good and bad dictators. And all the time he was relating the story of Moses.

About mid-morning the church door opened and a young man entered. The students were diverted from their lessons and welcomed this interruption.

'It is Emile,' whispered Maria.

The young man was extremely good-looking. He removed his hat and walked over to the old priest. Father Sebastian looked up with a slight frown at this interruption. The frown disappeared and was replaced by a welcoming smile.

'Emile, you have come to confess your sins. I hear you have been leading the girls of the town a merry dance.'

Emile blushed. 'No Father, I have done with all that frivolity. I have come to ask you to marry me.'

There was a buzz of excitement amongst the children. Emile was obviously a well-known and popular figure. The young girls were looking on in admiration as he stood blushing and twisting his hatbrim in his hands. The old priest was looking at his former pupil with a wistful smile on his wrinkled face.

'What wonderful news! I am glad you have decided to settle down at last. And who is the lucky girl?'

'Miranda Diaz, Father.'

'My boy.' The priest stood and moving forward embraced Emile. He held him at arm's length. 'It will give me the greatest pleasure to perform the marriage ceremony. When is the happy event to take place?'

'Next week, Father, if you can fit us in.,

'Of course, of course! We will make it a day to remember.'

As they walked back from the church towards the monastery Father Sebastian filled in Brother Joseph on Emile's background.

'He was always very wild and mixed with a crowd of troublemakers, I suspect he was involved in cattle-rustling and sheep-stealing. It was even rumoured that he was running with Gomez Farias and his gang of robbers. There was talk of some trouble with Gomez and that is why he came back to the village. Some say it was over a woman. Emile was always one for the girls. Anyway, whatever the problem I think it frightened Emile and he returned to his family. He got a job as a *vaquero* with Eugene Diaz, one of the big landowners. Miranda is his youngest daughter. Emile works hard and saves his money and now he wants to marry.

'Miranda Diaz is the local beauty. She has an elder sister Anna, who is very proud and also very beautiful. I suppose Miranda could have any man in the locality. However she has chosen Emile. They will make a handsome couple. Her father will spare no expense to give them a good wedding. It will be a day to remember.' The priest glanced sideways at his companion. 'A wedding is a festival for these villagers. It is full of music and colour and singing and dancing. I shall ask our superior if you can assist me at the marriage ceremony. I think you will enjoy the spectacle.

'This Gomez Farias, where does he hang out?' Brother Joseph asked.

'Some say he has a hideout in the Linaloas. He makes regular raids on gold shipments from the Sahagun Mines. Gomez Farias is very bad. He has killed many men. It is said Gomez never forgives an insult and never forgets a grudge. It surprised everyone that Emile had a run-in with him and was allowed to come back here and settle down peacefully. The trouble between them must not have been too serious. Otherwise Gomez would have exacted a brutal revenge on Emile. That Gomez, he is a very terrible man.' The old priest crossed himself. 'He is evil. May God have mercy on my soul for saying such a thing about a fellow human being, but I have heard so many terrible things about him.'

They walked on in silence after this exchange — the old priest and the young golden-haired novice.

12

It was as Father Sebastian had intimated. The wedding of Emile Macon and Miranda Diaz, as far as the town was concerned, was the event of the century. No one could remember such an ideal marriage.

Emile was dark and handsome with perfect white teeth and a good-humoured pleasantry that endeared him to all who made his acquaintance. His bride to be, Miranda, was a startlingly beautiful young woman with high cheekbones, lustrous dark hair and a smile that enslaved all who met her.

Dressed in an immaculately laundered white suit, Emile waited inside the church on the day of the wedding. He patted constantly at his dark hair which had added lustre from an aromatic oily dressing, and smiled nervously at Brother Joseph.

Father Sebastian knelt before the altar with head bowed. He was dressed in the colourful vestments that denoted his role as the priest who would perform the wedding mass and marriage ceremony. His acolyte, Brother Joseph was standing to one side patiently waiting to assist at the service.

The brother nodded reassuringly at the nervous young Mexican. The monk had a lean handsome face that was not quite so pretty as Emile's. A livid scar from an incident in his former life ran along his temple and gave him a slightly dangerous look. The scar suggested either a brutal accident or a wound sustained in conflict. In fact the scar was a badge earned in his former life as a United States lawman. For Brother Joseph the scar was an unpleasant and constant reminder of a past he was trying to put behind him. Brother Joseph was formerly Deputy Joe Hammer. Now he was simply Brother Joseph.

The church was packed with most of the population of San Christobel.

Portly matrons assiduously told their rosaries with lowered eyes that missed nothing. Nut-brown children fidgeted incessantly, restrained in their pews only by the hissed threats of their elders. Everyone wore his or her finest attire. The children were scrubbed clean and the girls had pretty ribbons holding their hair in place. Along the side of the church beneath the Stations of the Cross was crowded the overspill of eager people for whom there was no room in the pews.

The peons from the surrounding countryside, anticipating an excuse for a day of indulgence, had swollen the congregation. As a consequence there was a vast mix of people in the town for the festivities.

With so many people in the church the heat was building like the inside of a slow oven. Windows had been prised open in an attempt to ease the stifling atmosphere. The sturdy wooden doors were gaping so that Brother Joseph had only to raise his eyes and he could look out on to the hard-packed earth of the town plaza.

Beneath his simple woollen robes Brother Joseph sweated and allowed his mind to drift. For a few tempting moments he allowed himself to imagine what he would be doing now if he had not found the peace and solitude of the monastery at San Christobel.

He thought of his old comrade in arms. Herbie Banner and wondered idly how the deputy was faring. Herbie had been concerned his son Forrest wanted to follow in his footsteps and become a lawman. Herbie wanted something better for his son and he was right. The life of a lawman was no life. He only hoped Forrest would obey his father's wishes and become a lawyer and not a lawman.

Maybe I should have followed that path, he mused.

But at the time he would not have been content with such a sedentary life. He yearned for the excitement of the chase and the danger that ensued when he pursued and confronted the law-breakers. There had been idealism then, too.

I had wanted to make the land safe for decent people, he recalled.

But the killing had become an inherent part of Deputy Hammer's duties. The ghosts of the men he had slain would not rest. The nightmares had been insistent and in despair he had fled the life of bloodletting. Someone else had that task now, he thought. His mind came back to the present and he contemplated what he had achieved since arriving at San Christobel.

It had taken a few months for the terrifying dreams to subside. Even now he would wake occasionally in a night sweat with the ghouls from his bloody past parading through his dreams. He wondered if they would ever fade, or would they haunt him to the grave?

I will do my penance on earth, he

mused. By burying myself in this obscure Mexican town I have severed all links with my violent past. Perhaps God will forgive me for the terrible deeds I have committed.

'*Come all ye sinners unto me. I have washed away the stain of sin by the blood of the lamb,*' he prayed and hoped it was true.

From his position at the altar Brother Joseph could see a flutter of agitation among the peasants waiting out in the plaza in the hot sun. It rippled through the congregation like a gentle wind stirring through a cornfield. The men were pulling off their hats as a sign of respect. Women in colourful Indian costumes were raising their hands in adulation. Brother Joseph sighed again. It looked as if the long wait was over. The carriage of the Diaz family was arriving.

Sensing the change in the attention of the crowd Father Sebastian rose to his feet and turned to face the congregation. His hand rose in benediction and the people bowed their heads to receive the blessing. The wedding of Miranda Diaz and Emile Macon was about to begin.

13

The joyous sounds of music and dancing echoed through the narrow streets of San Christobel. The plaza in front of the church was a swirling mass of colourfully dressed people. Any Mexican community with pride in its achievements had a brass band and San Christobel was no exception.

The band members looked imposing in their freshly laundered uniforms and peaked caps. Lustily they blew on their instruments and banged on drum and cymbal. Tables had been set up on the edges of the plaza and these were dispensing chilli-enhanced dishes, tacos and enchiladas. These culinary delights were washed down with pulque, the local fiery drink.

Children ran through the crowds and begged continually for food at the stalls. One long table was set high up on a temporary wooden platform. Draped across the table were generous coverings. At this place of honour sat the newly-weds, looking flushed and happy. On each side of the smiling couple were seated the respective members of their families.

Also at the table were the soberly garbed figures of Brother Joseph and Father Sebastian. It had taken all the persuasive powers of Don Eugene to get the old priest to sit at the table of honour.

'It is for you and your families to sit there. I will only prevent you from enjoying yourselves. Eat, drink and be merry. I will kneel in the church and pray for your future happiness.'

But Don Eugene was not easily put off.

'Father Sebastian, you have taught both these children in your little school. Now today you have married them. It is fitting that you sit with us as a sign that God smiles on this holy union.'

Brother Joseph watched the old priest

and observed he ate sparingly and would drink only water, refusing the fine wines that were on offer at the wedding table. He followed suit and limited himself to experimenting with the various dishes. His palate was not used to the hot spices used in Mexican cooking. He eyed with some yearning the glasses of wine being quaffed by the revellers.

I still have sinful desires, he thought.

Since Father Nostrill had asked him to consider beginning the steps that would take him towards ordination and the priesthood he had wrestled with his carnal desires. Somehow, now that he was in a position to make that decision, the lure of worldly desires seemed to beckon with ever increasing temptation.

In my old life of sin and blood I took my pleasures as the urge arose, he mused to himself. When I needed a woman I found a willing companion for my lusts. I imbibed alcohol and I used my weapons to kill the ungodly. The most heinous crime of all was the taking of life.

As he contemplated these facts the explosions jerked him back to the present. He half rose from his seat in a sweat of anticipation, as if his old life had never gone away.

'Relax, Brother Joseph, it is only the fireworks. We always have fireworks at festive times.'

Self-consciously, Brother Joseph sat down. Without thinking he picked up a glass of dark-red wine and took a long draught. The drink was dry and spicy and reminded him of the wild strawberries he had picked as a child. He sat and stared at the drink somewhat confused. In a moment of forgetfulness he had broken his vow to abstain from intoxicating liquor.

It is a wedding, after all. I shall have to confess my sin to Father Nostrill, he thought.

Recklessly he picked up the glass and drained it. Beside him Don Eugene was smiling broadly as he refilled the young monk's glass.

'Drink up, Brother Joseph. Today I

lose a daughter but gain a fine son. It is a time of celebration and happiness.'

The fireworks seemed to be getting louder. People were smiling and looking up as the noise grew.

He saw the horsemen then. They were riding into the plaza seemingly heedless of the safety of the carousing dancers. Brother Joseph sat bolt upright. The men were firing pistols in the air. The explosions he had mistaken for fireworks had indeed been gunshots.

He watched the sombreros converging on the wedding table. People were screaming and running to avoid being crushed by the horses ploughing through the crowds. Some of the slower members of the community were elbowed aside or tripped and fell and disappeared beneath the trampling feet.

'The parting of the waters in the Red Sea,' he muttered as the wine took effect. 'Moses commanded the waters to part. The Jews crossed the dry bed of the sea. Behind them came the Pharaoh's forces into the seabed. Once the Jews were across safely, the waters flooded back. Pharaoh and his army were drowned.'

Beside him there was a sudden disturbance as some of the guests at the wedding table stood and shouted to the horsemen.

'It's a disgrace!'

'Who are those gatecrashers anyway?'

'Don Eugene, who invited these rude men? Send them away at once.'

All the shouting and protests were in vain. More and more of the horsemen forged into the plaza. The festive crowd, that moments before had been dancing and singing, was now fleeing in panic. They crowded into the side streets to get away from the prancing, bucking horses. As the noise and confusion of the fireworks and firearms panicked the animals they kicked and reared. Some of the revellers did not make it safely but were mown down by the plunging animals. Women and men and children were screaming.

By now all at the main table were on

their feet staring in horror as the scene of mayhem was enacted before them. Brother Joseph was standing with them, staring in bewilderment as the chaos grew. The horsemen drew closer and closer to the wedding table. It became clear this was their objective, for a cordon was formed in a semicircle around the front of the table. Brother Joseph stared out with the feeling that something terrible was about to happen.

14

One of the riders pushed his mount forward. He stood out from his companions because of his distinctive appearance. He had a broad chest and shoulders. A small head with bronzed, fleshy face topped the muscular body. Small, mean, black eyes were set beneath thick black eyebrows.

'Emile, it is I, your old friend and companion, Gomez.'

Brother Joseph glanced sideways at Emile. The newlywed was still sitting by the side of his wife. His face was deathly white as he stared with a horrified expression at the rider.

'You remember me — Gomez Farias!' the man continued cajolingly. 'We rode together in Concoctas. We robbed and killed and drank tequila together. They were good times, Emile.'

'Go from here at once!'

Don Eugene was on his feet. Like his new son-in-law his face was pale but it was the white of anger. He was a stout man with grey hair and a heavy, silver-tinged beard.

'Can't you see this is a wedding celebration — a day of peace and happiness. Now go from here and take your ruffians with you.'

There was a large pistol stuffed into the bandit's sash. Casually he plucked it from its resting place and pointed it at Don Eugene. There were no preliminaries, no warnings as the shot rang out. Don Eugene collapsed back into his chair as the bullet struck him. His face was grey and shocked as he stared in disbelief at the man who had shot him. Women screamed and the men stepped back a pace. All around the wedding table was a hubbub of agitation as the guests cowered before this display of brutality.

'Father!' screamed Miranda Diaz.

She jumped to her feet and pushed past the terrified guests to the wounded

116

man's side. He was sitting grey-faced, with his hands clasped to his midriff. His wife was sitting rigid with shock beside her husband, afraid to move. Her daughter's action roused her from her inertia. She rose to her feet and the two women grabbed napkins and pressed them against the wound. Blood was staining Don Eugene's hands and clothes. Gomez ignored the women.

'Now where was I before that old goat interrupted! Oh yes, Emile, my good friend. You did not invite me to your wedding. That was very bad. I was much hurt. Did you forget your old friends? We missed you from around our campfires.' He was casually leaning forward on his saddle, his pistol making small movements as he talked. 'But you do not seem glad to see me. You sit there so pale and quiet. Is it the wine! Perhaps you have drunk too much!'

'Gomez,' Emile croaked at last. 'I never meant to slight you. I did not think you would want to come into San Christobel for my miserable wedding.'

The bandit chief smiled at Emile and shrugged.

'For an old friend I would come through hellfire to help make his wedding day one to remember.'

By now the plaza had emptied of revellers. The space where the dancers had pranced and cavorted was now occupied by a band of armed horsemen. Only the bandits and the people at the main table were left in the square.

'I come mainly for my gold, Emile. The wedding was only an excuse. When you left with Conchita the gold went also. I was much hurt, Emile. But all is fair in love and war. I loved Conchita but I loved the gold more. So if you give my gold back to me I shall go back to my hills again, you can carry on with your wedding and everyone is happy, no?'

'For the love of God!' A new voice broke in.

There was the scraping noise of a chair being pushed back. Brother

Joseph had been sitting very still awaiting developments. He recognized the voice of Father Sebastian.

'This is a holy day for these families. Take your brood of devils back where they came from.'

Brother Joseph watched the bandit chief. Gomez flicked his eyes towards the priest, a frown of annoyance on his cruel face.

'Shut up old man! Save your ranting for the old maids and children who believe in your superstitions.'

'I will not shut up, you ungodly creature.'

A rifle blasted into the silence of the plaza. Father Sebastian was punched backwards as the bullet hit him in the chest. He became entangled in his chair and disappeared behind the table.

Women began screaming. In spite of the guns aimed at the top table Brother Joseph rose swiftly and pushed past the frightened guests towards the stricken priest. Another shot rang out and something flicked at the brother's robe.

He ducked behind the table and crawled towards his wounded companion.

'Stop firing!' Gomez was yelling. 'Antonio, don't you know its bad luck to kill a priest?'

Brother Joseph had reached Father Sebastian. Blood was darkening the front of his habit. Turning quickly to the table he grabbed up a carving knife and began to hack at the material. The old priest was staring up at his helper. His breathing was coming in short shallow bursts.

'I think I will go to my God shortly,' he murmured. 'I want you to carry on the teaching, Brother Joseph.'

The young monk ignored the priest's remarks. He had cut away the tunic and was packing napkins into the wound. The material soaked up the blood at an alarming rate.

'I'll get a cart and take you back to the monastery,' he panted. 'Brother Augustine will soon patch you up.'

'God is calling me, Brother. I have

tried to live a good life. I do not fear death.'

Brother Joseph's hands and sleeves were covered in blood as he worked on the wound. A red rage was building in him. Two elderly men on a day that should have been a day of joy, shot down like animals. The priest's head lolled to one side and Brother Joseph, who had seen more dead men than he wanted, knew his friend had died. The tears flowed as he stared at that grey old head. He could not help it. There lay a gentle old priest who had only wanted to teach children in order to prepare them for life. He could hear the voices and movement around him but he had only eyes for the dead man.

'Goodbye, Father.'

He began to say the prayers for the dead over the blood-soaked corpse of his friend and mentor.

15

As the young monk knelt by the dead priest he could hear someone shouting. It was the bandit chief. He was uttering some sort of ultimatum. Slowly Brother Joseph looked up and listened. He could not have explained why he did it but he slipped the knife he had been using to cut Father Sebastian's robes inside his own robe. Gomez had dismounted and was strutting among the terrified guests.

'If you won't give me my gold, Emile then I shall have to take something you value maybe more than the gold.'

He had reached the weeping Miranda, crouched by her wounded father. His hand reached out and he grabbed a handful of her luxurious hair. He dragged the girl against him and planted a rude kiss on her lips.

She moaned and struggled against him. Her fists hammered on his shoulders. She was no match for his brute strength. The bandit chief left off kissing and threw back his head and laughed.

'By God, you can certainly pick them, Emile. This one is full of fire. I think she likes me.' He laughed again.

'Gomez please, she is my wife. We've just been married.'

'I like her. I think I will marry her myself. I have not been married before. I had a woman once. Her name was Conchita. I loved that woman very much. I think I might have married her. But I never got the chance to ask her. My good friend Emile took her away from me. My pride, it was wounded. How could you do such a thing, Emile?'

'Please Gomez, not Miranda,' Emile pleaded. 'It is a sin to covet another man's wife. Whatever Conchita and I did she was not your wife.'

Gomez still held the girl tight against him. He was smiling thoughtfully.

'Have you consummated the marriage, Emile?' he said slyly.

'Of course not! We have just been married but an hour or so.'

'You obviously do not know your canon law, Emile.' He suddenly remembered Brother Joseph. 'Priest, come here.'

Slowly the young monk raised himself up and walked over as he was commanded. The girl hung weeping, restrained by the bandit's strong ann.

'Father, when a marriage is not consummated is it a real marriage?'

The young religious brother stared with implacable eyes at the bandit and remained silent. Gomez casually raised his pistol and fired a shot into a young man sitting along the table. The bullet hit him in the head and he went over backwards blood and brains spilling on to the platform. Women began screaming again.

'Each time you do not answer, Padre, I shall shoot someone. When no one is left then I will shoot you.'

'The Catholic Church decrees that in order for a marriage to be legal the marriage partners must complete the physical union.' Brother Joseph spoke steadily. There was no tremor in his voice — no sigh of fear. 'Only then is the marriage legal in the eyes of God.'

Smiling triumphantly Gomez turned to Emile.

'If I take your wife before you . . . how did the good priest put it, complete the physical union, then she is not legally married to you. I will be free to marry her myself.'

Emile said nothing, staring with stricken eyes at the bandit chief. Beside them stood Brother Joseph. His hand was across his chest and he felt the shape of the blade he had secreted beneath his robe.

I cannot use it, he thought regretfully. I am a man of God. I have renounced violence.

Yet he stared with cold eyes at the bandit and he was hard put not to take the blade and plunge it into the black heart of the man before him.

'I will be generous, Emile. You give me my gold and I will renounce my offer of marriage to the lovely Miranda. Though it will break my heart to do so.'

'Gomez, listen to me. I never got the gold. Conchita used me to help her transport the gold. She ditched me and I never saw her again. It is she you want, not me.'

The gun in the bandit's hand came up then and centred on Emile. Brother Joseph saw the finger tighten on the trigger.

'You lie!' he hissed.

'Emile,' a voice called out weakly.

Gomez swivelled round and stared at the man who had spoken. It was Don Eugene. His wife was kneeling by his side and holding the bloodstained napkins against his wound.

'Go to my hacienda.' Don Eugene was struggling to speak. 'Take my wife with you. She knows where we keep our money. Bring back the money and pay this vulture his price.'

A broad grin spread on the bandit's face.

'An excellent idea. At last we are getting somewhere. Mariano, take ten men. Go with this she-goat and bring back the money. We will wait here till you get back. If you do not return within the hour we will kill everyone in the town. Vamoose!'

It was soon arranged. The band of men rode out on their mission with the frightened wife of Don Eugene.

'Let us join in the festivities,' called Gomez. 'It is time to join the wedding feast.'

His men needed no second bidding. They whooped in delight, let off their weapons in a thunderous barrage and dismounted. They helped themselves to the food and drink abandoned by the townsfolk when they fled the plaza. Gomez kicked a plump merchant and his wife from their chairs.

'Come, Miranda, you and I will get acquainted while we wait. Padre, come sit on the other side of me. We will discuss philosophy and other weighty matters. It is long since I talked to an educated man. Even though you are a priest you will have to do.'

The bandit put a bottle of wine to his lips and drank. The members of his gang were roughly displacing the guests of honour and pushing them into the plaza. There was a mixture of young and old amongst the uprooted guests. They hung around in the plaza, scared and bewildered.

'Dance!' yelled a bandit and fired his pistol into the earth at the feet of an elderly matron.

His companions took up the game and encouraged the guests to dance for their entertainment. They roared encouragement and fired at the feet of the guests. It was harrowing to watch the crowd of elegantly dressed people cavorting around as bullets thudded into the ground, raising puffs of dust with the impact. The bystanders could only look on helplessly. Joe Hammer sat by the bandit chief and held his anger in check.

'I am a man of God,' he murmured. 'I have renounced violence.'

He repeated this over and over. Each time he repeated the mantra he did so with less and less conviction.

16

'There is something about you, Priest, that bothers me.' Gomez looked at the man in the monk's robes with a perplexed expression. 'You don't seem to be afraid of me. Your holy brother lies dead and yet you sit beside me without a tremor. Aren't you afraid that you may be next to die?'

Joe Hammer steadily regarded the bearded bandit. Before he could respond Gomez pulled his pistol and shoved it into his face. Hammer sat very still as he felt the round muzzle of the weapon pressing hard into his cheekbone.

'If I pull this trigger your skull will disintegrate as the slug bores through your head and out the other side. What do you say to that, Priest?'

'The moment we leave our mother's womb we start the process of death,' Hammer replied with no indication the gun pressing into his face bothered him. 'It may take six days or six months or sixty-six years. Death is as sure as the sun rising in the morning or setting at night. I may die before you, and then again, you may go first.'

'You are not as priests I have known. What were you before you became a priest?'

'I was a peacemaker. I would pursue wicked men and try to persuade them to give up their lives of evildoing.'

'You what? Surely that was a dangerous activity! It's a wonder you never got your God-bothering head blown off.'

'I will admit there were times it was touch and go. However, in the end I usually managed to persuade the malefactors to see the error of their ways. God watched over my work and helped me.'

'You're a weird priest. Don't pull any of that holy mover palaver with me. As you can see by your dead brother, we don't hold priests in much regard.'

'Don't worry, I will respect your wishes. God works in mysterious ways. I may be the instrument of your salvation, or then again, you might save me. Like a bolt out of the blue something may stab you to the heart and change your whole outlook on life and death.'

Gomez stared at Hammer with a puzzled expression.

'You trouble me. Priest. I have a feeling I should just shoot you and be done with it. I'll think on it. Start saying your prayers in case I might do what my instinct tells me to do and shoot you out of hand.'

'I'll certainly prepare myself for that event, my friend.'

He joined his hands together and bowed his head in prayer. All around Hammer could hear the bandits becoming louder and louder. They kept up a steady barrage of shots at the unfortunate dancers in the plaza. Either because they were becoming inebriated or were deliberately targeting the dancers, a few were being hit by wildly flying bullets. Some of the bandits had taken up positions by the band and by threatening them with their guns were encouraging them to keep playing.

For the time being Gomez lost interest in Hammer and turned his attention to the girl by his side. He pulled her close and began pawing and kissing her. She struggled against him. The more she fought him the more his ardour increased.

A few places along the table Emile sat white-faced and shrunken in his chair as the day that should have been the happiest day in his life became a living nightmare. It was a terrifying ordeal as well for the wedding guests, as they endured the shooting practice of the hard-drinking bandits.

When at last the bandits returned there were a few extra bodies bleeding into the dust of San Christobel. Mariano rode his big stallion through the capering dancers and hauled up opposite his chief. There was a broad grin on his face as he tossed a couple of heavy sacks on to the table in front of Gomez.

'Gold, *amigo*. I did not count it but there is plenty.'

Gomez pulled the drawstring and plunged his hand inside. The glint of gold could be seen between his fingers as he withdrew his clenched fist. He opened his hand and a glittering cascade of gold coins poured back into the mouth of the sack.

'It seems our Don Eugene is a rich man. No wonder you wanted to marry his daughter, Emile. Very good. This is what we came for, eh Mariano!'

'*Sí*, it is good.'

There was a sudden commotion in the plaza. Gomez and his lieutenant looked up at the disturbance. A bandit in a wide sombrero was seen charging his horse through the plaza with complete disregard for the pedestrians trapped within the square. He knocked down at least two people with his reckless riding.

'Gomez!' the man yelled as he hauled his sweating mount to a halt beside Mariano. 'Soldiers heading this way.'

'Mariano,' Gomez snapped. 'Get the men assembled. We must leave immediately. Take the gold with you.'

As his lieutenant leaned forward to recover the sacks of gold the men within earshot were already racing for their mounts. Gomez turned his attention back to the remainder of his frightened audience clustered round the wedding table.

'Emile, I have decided to renege on my original proposition. I will marry your lovely Miranda. But in order to make it entirely legal I will make her into a widow first.'

That deadly pistol was coming up. Emile, seeing and hearing the bandit's threat, half-rose in his seat, terror on his face.

'No, Gomez,' he screamed and put his hands up before him as if he could ward off the bullets.

As the bandit chief fired Hammer

threw himself at the gunman. He cannoned into Gomez and pushed him off balance. They both went down in a tangle of table coverings. Plates and bottles crashed to the floor along with the struggling men. Brother Joseph had one hand on the pistol while his other gripped the bandit's throat. A sudden and paralysing agony radiated out from his groin as Gomez drove his knee up with brutal force. The monk grunted in pain but hung on grimly.

'I knew I should have killed you, Priest.' The hate-crazed face of the bandit chief glared up at him. Straining against Brother Joseph's grip on his pistol Gomez tried to bring the weapon to bear on his assailant. It was an evenly matched contest. Gomez was brutally strong while Hammer was wiry and muscular. For moments they strained, oblivious of the turmoil around them as the bandits, seeing their entertainment cut short, grabbed jewellery and any other loot they could gather from their victims.

When they went down Hammer had managed to land on top of Gomez. The agony in his groin was easing slightly as he strained to prevent the bandit chief from bringing his pistol round to get a shot at him. Their faces were inches apart as they fought. With a suddenness that took him completely by surprise Gomez let go the pistol. With all resistance gone Hammer's hand slammed down on the boards of the platform, bruising his knuckles painfully. The pistol bounced a few feet to the side. At the same time as he let go Gomez clenched his fist and drove a hard punch into his assailant's face. Hammer grunted and tried to reach for the discarded pistol. He never made it. It felt as if the table had collapsed on the back of his head and he lost consciousness.

Gomez stared up at his lieutenant. Mariano was grinning down at his boss. In his hand he held one of the sacks of gold coins he had brought back from the Diaz hacienda.

'I know how the priests of our

benighted land like gold,' he said.

Gomez stood and recovered his pistol. With a vicious snarl, he aimed it at the monk's head.

'No, Gomez, you said yourself: killing priests is bad luck. We killed one and already the soldiers are on our tail. If you kill this one also, who knows what misfortune will befall us?'

For long baleful moments Gomez stared down at the unconscious man.

'All my instincts are telling me to kill this priest, but perhaps you are right. I will let him live for now. Perhaps we will come back another day and then I can kill him.'

When he had holstered his pistol, he kicked the comatose body. Raising his boot he stamped down hard on the monk's head. His brutal spur cut a deep gash in the unconscious man's cheek.

'When he wakes he will have something to remember me by. Let's go. Bring the woman. She is a widow now and will want consoling.'

He vaulted the table and mounted. Weeping bitterly Miranda, still dressed in her wedding dress, was dragged up behind Mariano. In quick time the plaza emptied of riders. They left behind a scene of carnage. Where there had been happy wedding celebrations now there was mourning and weeping as the townsfolk crept back to help the wounded and the dying.

17

Brother Joseph stood before Father Nostrill. The old priest sat quietly looking at his young postulant. A blood-stained bandage covered his gardener's head and part of his face.

'I was told you attacked the bandit leader, Gomez. Though some would applaud those actions I think it was ill-advised.'

'My actions came from anger. They shot Father Sebastian. Then Gomez was about to shoot Emile. I threw myself at him in an attempt to prevent another death.'

'In that you did not succeed. Emile has died since of his wound.'

'I am sorry. I did what I could.'

'A priest is a man of God. What example are you setting when you indulge in brawling with common criminals? You will have to rethink your whole attitude. I begin to wonder whether my first instincts about you were right and you were not suited to the holy discipline of monastery life.'

The monk stared steadily back at the priest.

'A few weeks ago you showed me the weapons I had deposited with you. I asked you to sell them and give the money to the poor. If they are still in your possession I will reclaim them.'

An expression of sorrow crossed the old man's face.

'I feared this day would come. Something told me you had come here to exorcise a demon from your soul. I can see I have failed you, my son. That demon still haunts you.'

'You have not failed, Father. It is I who have failed. Yesterday, when I watched Gomez gun down an old frail man whose only passion in life was to give the children in his charge a decent start in life, I realized there was great evil in the world. People like Father Sebastian and Señor Diaz and Emile and Miranda need to be protected from men like Gomez. That was what I did before I came here. I was a peace officer. The killing got too much for me. I thought I could leave it behind and live a peaceful life here in San Christobel.' His smile was bitter and regretful. 'God was patient with me. He allowed me to believe I could leave all that behind me. Now I know how misguided I was. Some time ago, it almost seems in another lifetime, someone called me the Hammer of God. I am an instrument of God's justice. I will take my weapons and go from here.'

'Do not go down this path, Brother Joseph. Make a fresh start. Perhaps it will work out this time.'

'I did try to make a fresh start, Father. I stuck it out for six months. Then Gomez came along. I must protect the innocent and punish the wicked. That is my true destiny. I know that now.'

'Where will you go, Brother?'

'I will go after Gomez and make him pay for the crimes he has committed.'

'You are one man. What can one man do against the power of Gomez? You saw how he rode into San Christobel with impunity. He has many men under him.'

'God will guide me. The soldiers are at Señor Diaz's hacienda. They are proposing to go after Gomez. I shall join forces with them. I am sure they will welcome the skills I bring them.'

'I see you are set on this course, Brother Joseph.'

The priest rose with a sigh and went to the chest to retrieve the bundle of weapons he had stored there for many months.

'Will you receive my blessing before you depart?' he asked as he handed the bulky, cloth-wrapped bundle across.

Hammer took the package from the priest and pressed it against his chest with both arms. He knelt on the floor and bowed his head.

'*Benedicat vos omnipotens Deus,*

Pater et Filius et Spiritus Sanctus,' the old priest intoned the blessing.

'Amen,' responded the young man kneeling before him.

★ ★ ★

Hammer trudged along the dirt track leading to the Diaz hacienda. He still carried the cloth-wrapped bundle containing his weapons — the instruments of death he had thought to forgo. Now he carried them under his arm, reluctant to hang them on his body in the final act of commitment. He heard the wheels of a cart coming up behind him. He turned and stopped while the cart drew level. The driver, who had a brown wizened face, hauled his mule to a halt.

'Padre.' The driver held a long switch in his hand he used to drive his mule. 'Are you walking as a penance or because you have no mule?'

'I have no mule. I need to get to the Diaz hacienda. Could I hitch a lift?'

'If the holy father will accept a lift in such humble company then climb aboard.'

Hammer carefully laid his bundle on top of the cargo of corncobs. Hitching up his robes he clambered into the cart beside the driver.

'Lucifer, hup hup!' the old man called and tapped the mule with his stick. The cart lurched forward. The driver looked shrewdly at his passenger.

'Are you the priest who fought with Gomez Farias?'

'Yes,' Hammer answered shortly.

There was a moment's silence before the old man continued:

'I was not there myself but many people are talking about it. They say you tried to save the life of Emile.'

Hammer said nothing. The old man was shaking his head.

'It was a terrible business. Gomez Farias is a very bad man. Señor Diaz is shot but they say he will recover. He is offering five thousand pesos to anyone who can rescue his daughter and another five thousand for the one who kills Gomez.' The man sighed. 'I do not suppose anyone will take him up on the offer.'

The man beside him made no effort to join in the conversation. He sat brooding — hardly taking notice of the countryside they were traversing. The driver rattled on but his travelling companion did not hear. He was reliving the terrible events of the previous day and wondering how he was to set off after the bandits with no horse, no proper clothes and only his pistols and knife to assist him. His hope was that the army would take him with them when they went in pursuit of Gomez. His information was that they were resting up at the hacienda before setting off after the bandits.

18

Captain Calleja had heavy black hair and a thin pencil-line moustache. He was a small man and his uniform had been tailored to fit his compact body. If the gold braid and decorative piping said anything about his soldiering abilities then he must have been one of the best. At that moment he was staring with some distaste at the dishevelled figure in the monk's robes before him.

'Padre, we do not carry passengers, especially priests. This is a dangerous mission we go on. Gomez has a small army of brigands with him. I cannot play nursemaid to a soft-bellied holy man.'

'I am no longer a priest,' Hammer said tightly, trying to rein in his temper. He had given up trying to explain that he was not a priest but only a lay brother. 'I was not always a holy man.

Before I joined the community at San Christobel I was an American lawman. I can handle a gun along with the best of them.'

'Padre, do not bother me. Go back to your church and if you think it will do any good pray for the success of our mission.'

With a look of contempt on his face the captain turned abruptly. As far as he was concerned the interview was terminated. Hammer stared angrily at the captain but the man was swinging up on to his mount. The soldier holding the reins saluted smartly and stepped back. Captain Calleja rode to the head of his column of soldiers. He nodded curtly to his sergeant. The second in command bawled the order to move out. Hammer watched helplessly as the horse soldiers paraded past him.

'Damn!' he said out loud.

Behind him someone coughed discreetly. He swung around and stared at a beautiful young woman gazing solemnly back at him.

'Luis told us he had given a lift to a monk. I don't suppose you would be that holy person he was speaking of?'

During his sojourn in the monastery the only female company Hammer had known were the youngsters he was tutoring at Father Sebastian's classes. Suddenly he was confronted with a female who was certainly more than a child. Not only was she female, she was also disturbingly beautiful.

Her long dark hair was cut in a fringe that almost but not quite obscured her eyes. She had flawless skin that was gently tanned to a delicate olive texture. From beneath her fringe of hair, dark wide eyes stared out at him steadily. For the first time in his life Hammer was struck dumb in the presence of female company.

'Is it customary for the holy brothers from San Christobel to use swear words and then stare rudely at young women?' she asked coldly.

Hammer swallowed hard before replying. 'I . . . I'm sorry, miss. I did not hear

149

you arrive. I certainly did not mean any offence.'

'My father has learned of your arrival. He wishes to speak to you. Follow me.'

The young woman turned abruptly and strode swiftly towards the house. She was dressed in a black riding outfit of tight trousers and a short jacket. Hammer could not take his eyes from her firm buttocks as he meekly followed.

The hacienda was opulent and spacious. It indicated vast wealth and resources. Don Eugene was propped up on cushions in a large, ornately furnished room. His skin looked waxy against the dense growth of his beard.

'Brother Joseph, I believe,' he greeted Hammer.

The girl stood beside her father with her hand on his shoulder.

'When I heard you were here I sent my daughter Anna to fetch you. I want to thank you for what you did yesterday. You were the only one to do anything to try and stop the bloodshed.'

'Unfortunately I did not succeed. Your son-in-law was killed along with several others. You yourself came near death when you were brave enough to stand up to Gomez.'

'Nevertheless you tried to stop it. I find it somewhat intriguing that a man of the cloth should attack a murderer.'

Hammer said nothing and after a while the wounded man spoke again.

'I was told you wanted to travel with Captain Calleja.'

'The captain refused my request.' Hammer's voice was bitter as he spoke.

'What was your reason for such a request? I see you were injured in the fight with Gomez. Surely a man of God would not want to pursue Gomez out of vengeance?'

The young man gingerly fingered the bandage on his face where Gomez's spur had gouged a deep wound.

'Don Eugene, I have given up my vocation at the monastery. At the time I went there I thought it better for me to hide away from wrongdoers. Yesterday's events showed me I was wrong. God wants me to work in a more direct way with sinners. I was hoping to join with Captain Calleja in his pursuit of Gomez and his gang. Unfortunately, the captain has other ideas.'

'What does that mean, padre?' the girl spoke for the first time. 'Work in a more direct way with sinners!' she said in a scornful voice. 'Men like Gomez are beyond redemption. You are a fool.'

Hammer stared impassively back at her but did not respond to her jibe.

'What will you do now?' Don Eugene asked.

Hammer shrugged. 'I shall try to follow the trail of the bandits as best I can.' He did not elaborate any further.

'What will you do in the unlikely event you catch up with Gomez?' Anna asked, the scorn still evident in her voice. 'Will you read him a psalm and ask him to give up his life of crime?'

The eyes that stared back at her were unnervingly bleak. Slowly Hammer unwrapped his bundle and revealed the gunbelt and holstered pistols. He hefted the rig in his hand.

'I will kill him,' he said simply. 'It is what I do best.'

There was a stunned silence after this announcement from the supposed man of God.

'What are you?' Don Eugene asked eventually.

'Before I entered the monastery at San Christobel I was a lawman. I worked for Judge Cordway in a place called Tiverton.'

'Were you a good lawman?' For the first time Don Eugene showed some animation.

'If you mean by good, did I bring in the men I was sent after, then I was not good.' Hammer ignored the girl's snort of derision. 'My problem was that the men I went after were brought in draped over their horses. I was judge, jury and executioner. Eventually the bloodshed got too much for me. I wanted out. So one day after a shootout with a gang of killers I got on my horse and rode south till I stopped at San Christobel. I thought I would find peace there. Gomez wiped out that illusion. He rode into San Christobel and killed an old priest whom I loved very much. When I saw him about to shoot Emile I knew this killer must be stopped. I tried and failed. I aim to wipe out that failure.'

Father and daughter soberly regarded the young golden-haired man with the bloody bandage.

'How are you called?' Don Eugene asked eventually.

'My name is Joe Hammer.'

'Is it the reward you are after?'

'If I succeed in killing Gomez you can give the reward to Father Nostrill at San Christobel. I will also try to bring back your daughter.'

'You know I have this crazy idea that you might just succeed in this foolish quest. Anna, tell Manuel to pick out two horses for Mr Hammer. Tell him also to find suitable clothes for him. Unless Mr Hammer wishes to pursue his quarry garbed in the robes of a Franciscan friar.'

19

She was glaring at him with barely concealed dislike. He tried to ignore her as he checked his weapons. It was with some relief he heard Manuel approaching. The *mayordomo* was leading two horses. They were fine mounts with broad chests and strong legs capable of carrying a man all day and still being able to break into a gallop if needed. He stood up and welcomed the man.

'Thank you, these are good stock you have chosen for me.'

Manuel was a thin, middle-aged Mexican with a long narrow nose. He walked with the bow-legged gait of a born horseman.

'They will stay the course, *señor*. The crew had a search for clothes that will fit you. We had a job, for our *vaqueros* are not so tall or so deep in the shoulders.'

'Thank you, I'm sure they'll be fine.'

He took the bundle and looked round uncertainly. Manuel pointed to a small hexagonal structure standing partly inside the gardens.

'You can use the gazebo to change.'

When he emerged again he was dressed in a pair of denims that were too short. His shirt strained at the buttons and the jacket felt tight under his arms. As well as all this, the boots pinched his toes. He had wrapped his sandals in the robe and he handed these to Manuel.

'Perhaps you can return these to the monastery sometime? I have no further use for them.'

'*Sí*, Señor Hammer.'

During these activities Anna Diaz had stood with folded arms and a disapproving look on her face.

'Perhaps I should say goodbye to Don Eugene and thank him for all his help?' Hammer queried.

'He is resting now,' the *mayordomo* replied. 'As you can appreciate, the shooting and the abduction of his daughter has weakened him considerably. He is not a young man any more. He asked me to give you this.'

Manuel handed over a small leather purse. Hammer could feel the hard shape of coins and looked up at the *mayordomo*.

'I do not know when I will be able to repay all this.'

'You can repay him by bringing back his daughter.' Manuel offered his hand. '*Adios, señor* and good luck.'

Hammer watched him walk away with the rolling stride so characteristic of a man who spends all his working hours in the saddle.

'We will never see you again.' Anna's voice was contemptuous, with a suppressed anger. 'You have fooled my father into giving you a grubstake and now you will run back to your precious Tiverton. What we have given you is probably more wealth than you have ever seen in your odious little life. Swindling money and goods from a wounded man grieving for his daughter is the act of a despicable piece of vermin.'

For the first time since leaving the big house he turned and looked directly at her. His own anger was building and he could not refrain from biting back at her.

'It strikes me you're doing everything to dissuade me from going after Gomez. It's almost as if you don't want your sister rescued. Did she upstage you by marrying Emile and leaving you on the shelf? Is that why you don't want her back?'

She was quick as a cat but not quick enough as her hand came up to slap him. He grabbed her arm and pulled her close. Then he did what he had wanted to do since his first sight of the gorgeous Anna. He kissed her.

It was a hard and fierce meeting of lips. This was the first woman he had been close to in many long, guilt-ridden months. He poured all his passion and frustrations out in that encounter. His body was hard and rigid against her softness. She struggled in his embrace. It was of no avail. She could not break away from that stretched-out, brutal kiss.

Abruptly he released her. She staggered back, her face a mask of fury. Even as she spat out her anger he thought how beautiful she looked. For a moment they stood glaring at each other, both breathing heavily.

'You are the most desirable creature I have ever encountered,' he said before she could speak. 'You are spoiled and arrogant and some man needs to take you and put you across his knee and spank some humility into you. If your sister still lives I will bring her back to your father or die in the attempt. Whether I survive or not, it does not matter. Either way I will prove you wrong in your opinion of me.'

Before she could make reply he was in the saddle. Without looking again at her he jigged his horse forward and with the packhorse trailing he started away.

She stared after him. Slowly her hand came up and she touched her lips with her fingers. She remembered the anger in that kiss and wondered at it. He was right about one thing. No man had ever treated her in such a callous and offhand manner. Men tended to step warily around her, awed by her beauty and her position as the elder daughter of Don Eugene.

Conflicting emotions of anger and doubt and uncertainty surged through her as she stared after the retreating form of Joe Hammer. She shivered, though the day was hot, and put her arms around her body and hugged herself. Then she made the sign of the cross.

'May God and his holy angels keep you safe, Joe Hammer. And bring you and Miranda home safe.'

As he left the ranch he saw a figure waiting on the trail. Joe Hammer touched the pistol strapped to his waist. It was an automatic gesture and came from years of watching for danger in every encounter. Old habits were reasserting themselves. Joe Hammer was on the move. Joe Hammer was once again the hunter and rode with the hunter's caution, As he drew closer he recognized the *mayordomo*.

'Manuel?' He noticed the bedroll tied on the back of the horse and waited for the man to speak.

'*Señor*, you will require a guide.'

It was not a question but a statement. Hammer waited.

'I was godfather to Miranda. I could not live with myself if I stayed here and did nothing.'

'What did Don Eugene say when you told him he would have to manage without his *mayordomo*?'

Manuel looked away. 'I did not tell the don. He would not have permitted me to go.'

'You know there is a more than evens chance we may not return?'

Manuel ignored this observation. 'What is your plan?'

'Plan!' Hammer ruminated for a

moment. 'I guess I'll just follow Gomez. When I catch up with him I'll beg him to release Miranda.'

'This is not a joking matter, *señor*. A young woman's life is in danger.'

'Yeah, well, the part about following Gomez is the core of the plan.' Hammer shrugged. 'What happens after that is in the hands of God.'

'You think you will find Gomez as easily as that? How do you think he has survived all these years? He has eyes and ears everywhere. Between Gomez and those who seek him there are layers of spies and informers. In every hamlet and every town there are men paid by Gomez to watch out for *rurales* and soldiers coming after him. He will melt into the hills and no one will find him if he does not want to be found.'

Hammer frowned at the *mayordomo*. 'How do you know so much about Gomez?'

There was a thin smile on the man's narrow face as he answered. 'I worked with Emile, rest his soul. We talked. I learn a lot from Emile.'

'I take it you have some ideas on how to overcome these obstacles?'

'There is a town called El Ventio. It services the needs of Oro Grande mines. If we are to get a lead on Gomez I suggest we start there.'

20

El Ventio was a picturesque colonial town roughly 500 miles north of Mexico City. It was situated in a relatively flat part of an undulating valley and divided by a tiny stream called the Madena, which wound through the town. The area was within easy riding distance of the foothills of the Sierra Madre. It was also within striking distance of the United States border. To the south of the town was the Franciscan monastery, Templo de la Cruz. It was towards this that Hammer and Manuel headed.

'I'll introduce myself as a friend of Father Nostrill, perhaps they will give us lodging for the night,' Hammer said to his companion. 'The brothers usually know what is going on in the area. We might get a lead on Gomez and his gang.'

At first Father Dominick was wary of the two travel-stained strangers. However, once he learned that Hammer had spent some months as a brother at the San Christobel monastery he welcomed them enthusiastically. He was especially keen for news of Father Nostrill who was an old friend. He was also curious as to what had led Hammer to give up his vocation as a brother. So he told Father Dominick about the fateful events at the wedding.

'I felt compelled to go after Gomez and try to undo some of the harm.'

'He shot poor Father Sebastian!' The priest crossed himself. 'I knew the good father. A man dedicated to God. May his soul rest in peace. Gomez is well known about here. He has a hideout somewhere in the mountains. His gang raids and pillages north and south of the border. From time to time they come into the town to buy supplies and patronize the cantinas and bordellos.' Again the priest crossed himself.

'What about the *rurales*?' Manuel

was moved to ask. 'Do they take no action against them?'

'*Rurales*!' The priest snorted. 'The men of the *rurales* are no more than bandits themselves. They are in the pay of Gomez. When army patrols appear from time to time the *rurales* warn Gomez and his gang and they fade back into the mountains. The army comes and the *rurales* lead it on fruitless searches for bandits. When the army finds nothing it goes back to barracks and Gomez resumes his robbing and killing. Pah!

'It is wicked times we live in. Perhaps the last times are coming. It is foretold in the holy Book that there will be wars and rumours of wars and men will commit wicked and selfish acts.' Father Dominick looked pityingly at his two guests. 'My advice is to return to your homes and forget about Gomez and his outlaws. There have been many sorties against him with combined operations of Americans and Mexican law officers. All have failed. Why? Because the people are afraid to inform on him. He is ruthless. You just told me how he arrived in San Christobel and meted out his punishment to your friend. That is how he is. He never forgets an insult or a hurt. He may bide his time but he will some day strike back. He is a vicious animal. Two men will accomplish nothing but their own deaths.'

'Thank you, Father, for your advice but I must make the effort. I owe it to Father Sebastian. Perhaps two will succeed where many have failed.'

The priest shook his head in resignation. 'Men, with their foolish and violent behaviour.'

'I will go into town and ask around to see if I can learn something to my advantage.'

'Do not go into town now, my young friend. It is getting late and the places of sin will be full to bursting with lost souls. There are men in El Ventio who will knife you for the price of a drink.'

'Sounds like a lot of places I've been,' Hammer replied. 'When men drink sometimes their tongues loosen.'

He didn't add that women also had the same tendency. Father Dominick would have been shocked to know that Hammer intended making up for his months of celibacy at San Cristobal when he went into El Ventio. The dens of iniquity the good father was warning him against sounded as good a place as any to start his quest for information.

Certainly, if the noise was any indication of the volume of sin in El Ventio Satan must have been rubbing his hands with glee. Hammer gigged his horse along the narrow streets looking for a likely place to begin his sinful activity. He chose the biggest and noisiest cantina. There was a corral round at the back of the building. As he dismounted a young boy appeared from out of the darkness.

'*Señor*, you want girl? My sister very pretty and very cheap.'

Hammer had no intention of wandering down some dark alley where no doubt a couple of men waited to pounce and rob him.

'I only have enough money for a drink,' he lied. 'I can't afford a girl and a drink.'

'American!' the boy exclaimed. 'I love American. Will you take me with you when you return to your own country.'

Hammer grinned through the gloom at the boy.

'I ride alone. When the US marshals chase me I would not have the time to care for a young boy.'

'You are an outlaw!' The boy sounded disappointed. 'My sister she would like to go to America.'

'If your sister is as pretty as you say then she should have no problem finding someone to take her to America.'

'I lied to you, señor. My sister is not pretty. Gomez had her branded.'

At the mention of the bandit chief's name Hammer tried to sound casual.

'Branded! I thought only cattle were branded. I never heard of women being branded.'

'She was Gomez's woman. But she fell in love with Captain Abascal. It is a tragic tale of love, *señor*.'

Hammer was intrigued. If she had been Gomez's woman perhaps he would be able to pump information from her.

'I would talk to your sister. Perhaps I can help. But I make no promises.'

'*Señor!*' The boy looked up expectantly. 'I will be your friend for life if you help us.'

'Lead on, you scallywag.'

After they had wended their way through a maze of narrow streets the boy stopped at a low-roofed adobe.

'I will take your horse around the back, *señor*. I will find him some hay. My sister, Conchella, is inside.'

The interior of the house was lit only by a couple of candles and a guttering fire. A woman was bending over the fire stirring a cooking-pot.

'Gabino, you are back early.'

Hammer cleared his throat. The woman instantly straightened up.

'Pardon, *señor*, I thought it was my brother Gabino. You seek entertainment? I can make you very happy.'

He looked for but could not see the branding scar the boy had told him of. Her eyes were wide-set and very dark. She had a strong straight nose and a full wide mouth. The overall impression was one of passion and sensuality.

She was looking at him in a curious sideways manner which he took to be simulated coyness. Then she was up close to him and he felt the heat of her body as she pressed against him. He could not speak for her lips were pressed hard against him. The banked-up fires from the months of suppressed desires at San Christobel welled up within him and burst into flame.

21

The bed was no more than straw-filled sacks. A curtain divided the bedroom from the living quarters. Waves of remorse swept through Hammer as he contemplated what he had done. The girl lying beside him was stroking his face.

'What is my good American thinking of?'

'I was thinking what kind of man would take a hot iron to a woman.'

It was only when he was fully committed in bed with her that he had felt the ridged flesh on the side of her face she had so artfully kept turned away from him.

He could detect the bitterness in her voice as she replied.

'Gomez is not a man. He is a devil.'

'I have heard of this Gomez. I hear men fear him and that is why he has never been arrested by the *rurales*.'

'Huh! The *rurales*! They are his paid dogs. When Gomez snaps his fingers they come running.'

A great sadness swept over him as he contemplated the terrible act committed on this lovely young girl.

'Why did he do this to you?'

She was silent for a moment then rolled over on her back. He lifted up on his elbow, resting his head on his hand, as he contemplated her lovely profile in the light from the single candle. This was her undamaged side — the side she always tried to keep turned towards him.

'I was Gomez's woman. He gave me freedom to come and go in El Ventio. One day whilst shopping in town I met a soldier. He was a captain. I was foolish. I fell in love with this beautiful captain. He looked so splendid in his uniform.'

She fell silent and Hammer waited, knowing it was a delicate moment for the woman. In a while she continued.

'He asked me to marry him. It was more than I ever expected. But I knew we had to be careful. If Gomez found out, his rage would be terrible. We made a date to elope and planned everything in detail. But that Gomez, he has eyes everywhere.' Her voice took on a note of bitterness. 'Nothing moves without his say-so. Lazaro hired a coach and I was to wait for him at the hotel. The coach arrived and I ran out to it. We did not get very far. Gomez was waiting a few miles out of town. He hanged Lazaro from a tree in front of me. I pleaded for his life and Gomez laughed at me.'

She suddenly turned her head and for the first time he saw the scar plainly. That beautiful face was a nightmare of disfigured tissue. The letter G was plainly burned deep into her cheek.

'Gomez told me no other man would have me and he was right. I have to live like this — a cheap woman in a cheap house.'

'So you want to leave El Ventio for

America and start afresh?' he asked gently, trying to keep the anger from his voice as he viewed the ruined face.

'That is not possible. Gomez will never let me leave. I tell that dream to Gabino to keep him in check, for I know his heart burns with vengeance. I am afraid he will one day do something foolish and try to harm Gomez. No one can touch that devil. So I tell him to bide his time and we will leave some day for a better life.'

She fell into a brooding silence. Hammer reached out and stroked her dark luxuriant hair.

'Do not give up hope. With so many people hating Gomez he will fall some day and you will be free of him.'

She smiled wanly at him but did not reply.

'Where does this Gomez hang out?' he asked casually.

Before she could respond there came a sharp cry from the other side of the dividing curtain. Hammer twisted around and groped for his discarded clothes.

176

He had placed the gunbelt with the garments and now he fumbled to extricate his gun from the bundle. The curtain was abruptly pulled aside and a dark figure loomed up in the opening. Hammer could see the gun in the man's hand.

Abandoning his search for his own weapon Hammer rolled fast into the man's legs. He hit hard and the gunman pitched over him and on to the girl. The gun went off as he fell and the girl screamed. Hammer was twisting back after the downed man. He clubbed hard with his fist into the man's neck. There was a grunt from the gunman but the blow did not disable him. He was trying to curl around and bring his gun to bear on his assailant. Hammer ignored the gun and punched again. This time he connected with the jaw hinge. The slugged man slumped and struggled feebly as the blow knocked the fight out of him.

Sensing the weakening of his victim Hammer made a lunge for the gun the man had been holding on to. As he was groping for the weapon he heard the yell of warning behind him. He rolled on his back bringing the weapon to bear. The movement saved his life. Suddenly shots were blasting into the sleeping compartment. Two dim forms were outlined in the gun flashes and he began firing back.

His shots slammed one of the gunmen backwards. His partner kept shooting. Hammer could hear bullets thudding into the man he had slugged. There was more screaming from the woman and then the second man went down.

Hammer began to scramble back across the bed. He had emptied the borrowed gun and now needed to find his own weapon. The bodies of the girl and the gunman were unmoving as he wriggled over. He had no time to examine them for he kept his eyes on the main room, expecting more gunmen. This time he had more success in finding his gunbelt. Keeping a wary eye on the room beyond he briefly examined the man and woman in the bed.

Conchella was lying with her eyes wide open. The side of her skull had been shattered. A dark mass of blood had spilled on to the bedding. He shuddered as he saw the wound. The bullet had entered the damaged side of her face and exited just above her ear. The man lying athwart her was dead also. His chest was a mess of blood. For a moment Hammer stared as he saw the uniform.

'*Rurales!*' he muttered

Hurriedly Hammer pulled on his clothing, silently cursing himself for being caught out. Fully clothed with his gunbelt strapped around him he cautiously moved out into the main part of the dwelling. A quick examination of the two gunmen sprawled on the dirt floor established they would do no more killing. A third body moved and moaned softly. With his gun at the ready Hammer moved across the floor and when he saw who it was he quickly holstered his gun.

'Gabino,' he called softly.

The boy opened his eyes and stared dazedly at Hammer.

'I tried to warn you, señor. They hit me on the head. It is very sore.'

'You're a very brave young man, Gabino.'

He helped the boy sit up. Gently he probed his head, seeking the wound. He found a large bump on the side of the boy's skull.

'Ah! No wonder you are sore. That's one helluva thump they gave you.'

He helped the boy to a rickety chair. With a quick movement he drew the curtains to the bedroom of the dead. Dazed as he was Gabino noted the action.

'My sister Conchella, is she all right?'

Back by the boy's side again, Hammer placed a hand on his shoulder. There was no easy way to do this.

'I'm sorry, Gabino, those men killed her. I did my best. I could not save her.'

The boy's tragic eyes stared up at him. 'Conchella,' he whimpered as the tears flowed. 'Conchella. I have no one now, *señor*. She was my only family.' Slowly he stood.

'Don't go in there, son. There is a dead man in there also. I will go and fetch help.'

'Help!' There was bitterness in the boy's voice now. 'No one in this town will help us. Gomez rules everything. They will be afraid to get involved.'

He walked over to the fallen policemen and stared down at the bodies. These were the men who had killed his sister. With a quick movement he kicked one of the bodies. Then he knelt and picked up a gun that had fallen to the dirt floor.

'I will find Gomez and kill him. It is the only honourable thing to do. Perhaps Conchella would still be alive if I had done something when Gomez hurt her. But I was only a boy then. Now I am a man and I have a gun. I will do this thing.'

'Gabino, listen to me. You know what these men are like. They are vicious killers,' Hammer said urgently not quite knowing how to handle this.

The boy looked no more than nine or ten years of age. Yet here he was with a gun in his hand talking about killing the most feared bandit in this part of Mexico. Even Hammer with all his experience of tracking criminals knew his own chances of catching up with Gomez were slim.

'One man will not accomplish this on his own. Whole squadrons of soldiers have tried to track him down. What can one boy with a pistol hope to accomplish? Come, I will take you to the mission. The fathers there will help you.'

For long unsettling moments the boy stared at him. The look in the boy's face was unnerving. It minded Joe Hammer of nothing more than a whipped dog. Tentatively he reached out a hand. The boy was quick. With no hint of his intentions he darted to the doorway and disappeared through it.

'Gabino!'

His shout was drowned out by the sudden blast of gunfire. Gabino came hurling back into the room. And then he was collapsing on to his back. Hammer stared in horror at the bloody ruin that had been the boy's chest.

22

The fusillade of shots continued from the front of the adobe. Bullets swept a leaden pathway through the small building and thudded into the mud walls, showering the floor with a jumble of plaster. The deadly hail plucked at the curtains separating the sleeping quarters from the main room. Some of the earthenware pots were shattered, adding to the clutter of debris on the floor. Voices were shouting out for those inside to surrender. There was no response to these orders. The firing petered out.

'OK,' a voice called. 'Get inside there and haul out any survivors.'

The silence was split asunder once more as guns were poked through the doorway and the policemen once again peppered the inside with shots. Two heads cautiously followed the guns.

Perceiving nothing to warrant any alarm the uniformed policemen advanced slowly, eyes and guns swivelling over the interior for movement that might indicate danger. Nothing moved in that room of death.

Gaining in confidence the men stepped further inside. All they could see were the corpses on the dirt floor. The bullet-riddled curtain separating the rooms gave them pause. They approached from each side and at an arranged signal whipped aside the ruined curtains to reveal two more bodies sprawled across the bedding. They stared with some curiosity at the naked body of the girl. Her head was a mess where a shot had shattered her skull. The men relaxed somewhat.

'All clear!' one of them called. 'They're all dead in here.'

Two more policemen entered.

'*Madre de Dios!*' The men crossed themselves. 'It is Conchella.'

'That is her brother Gabino — both dead.'

'Where is the American? We were told an American came here.'

'Maybe he left before we got here.'

'We better report this to Mariano. Something stinks here.'

'*Sí*, it's the smell of death. Let's go.'

When the policemen left, the silence of the tomb settled over the little adobe hovel where a young woman had tried to make a home for herself and her young brother. A young woman brutally mutilated by a savage bandit who was above the law and seemingly held the people of the region in a grip of fear. Now she and her brother lay dead, surrounded by some of the policemen who had murdered them.

The dead girl moved. For a few dreadful moments she heaved about and then rolled to one side. A man clambered out from the tangle of bedding. Breathing hard he sat for a few moments regarding the scene of carnage in the little adobe.

'Damn Gomez and all his hellish brood.'

He placed the girl in a more dignified position and draped some of the bed coverings over her. The body of the policeman he dragged into the inner room to join his two dead companions. Then he knelt beside the dead boy.

'I'm sorry, Gabino. If you hadn't rushed out when you did it might be me lying there. I promise you I will do my best to avenge you.'

Once more he checked his weapons, then stepped out into the night. Too late he saw the rifles aimed at him. He stopped abruptly and his body tensed as he expected a hail of lead to sweep him back into the house as had happened to Gabino. For tense, awful moments, he waited.

I should have stayed in San Christobel, he thought, and immediately dismissed the notion.

'Any move towards your weapons and my nervous men will blow you into so many bits we will have to scrape you up for burial.'

Hammer stood absolutely still. 'I am

a statue,' he said.

'Step forward one pace and lie face down on the ground.'

When he had done as he was told someone approached and frisked him. His hands were manacled and he was pulled to his feet.

'Bring him.'

Hammer recognized the man waiting at the police barracks.

He had every reason to remember Mariano from the fateful wedding day. Gomez's second in command was a handsome young man with carefully shaped close-cropped beard. There was a faint frown on his face as he regarded the prisoner.

'I know you, American. The last time I saw you you were a priest. You were trying your best to kill my good friend Gomez.'

'You are mistaken, friend. I was not trying to kill him. I just wanted him to repent of his evil ways.'

The bandit laughed. 'You are a strange one indeed, Padre. What are you doing here? It is a curious thing to find you in El Ventio. Have you followed us here?'

'I was hoping to find Miranda Diaz and return her to her father.'

Mariano's frown deepened. 'What sort of priest are you? I was told you went to a whore's house and then killed the policemen sent to arrest you. Has the Church decided that fornication and murder are no longer sins? If that is the case then I must inform Gomez immediately. I thought we were destined for hell but now perhaps we are not such evil men after all.'

Hammer was silent. Mariano's words bit deep. He was aware that everything the man said of him was true. He had fornicated and he had killed.

'Gomez wanted to finish you back in San Cristobel. He saw you as a threat and he wanted to eliminate you. I persuaded him not to. I believe now that Gomez was right. He has this instinct for survival that has served him well. There is something ominous about you turning up in El Ventio. I don't like it. My view of priests is that they are like vultures. They dress in black and are found hovering around the dead.'

While this conversation was going on the police captain sat in silence. Mariano glanced across at the policeman.

'What do you think, Captain?'

He received a shrug in reply. 'He looks like no priest I have ever seen. But then I have never met an American priest. Perhaps they do things differently there.'

The bandit stood. 'Take him out in the morning and shoot him. I have a feeling no one will come looking for him.'

Hammer stared at the retreating back of Gomez's lieutenant and wished he had a gun in his hand. The door closed behind Mariano and he was left alone with the police captain.

'Come, American. You have one night in my cells. In the morning my men will take you out and shoot you. You will have all night to make your peace with God.'

'What! You're gonna execute me on the command of a bandit! What about a trial? What has happened to the law in these parts?'

The smile the police captain gave was a trifle strained.

'You should count yourself lucky. Sometimes Gomez wants to interrogate prisoners. The bodies of such prisoners are delivered back for me to bury in the town cemetery. That, amigo, is not a nice thing to see. So just be grateful your fate in the morning is but a quick bullet. Count your blessings.'

'I need to see a priest. Can you send word to Father Dominick at the monastery?'

The police captain regarded his prisoner thoughtfully.

'Guards!' he yelled out.

Almost immediately two moustachioed young policemen entered the small office.

'Put this man in the cells and send someone out to the convent. Inform Father Dominick a prisoner requires the last rites.'

23

A raw young recruit brought him breakfast. He ate everything — goat's cheese and leathery tortillas accompanied by a jug of warm beer.

'The condemned man ate a hearty breakfast,' he muttered to his empty cell.

He lay on his bunk and contemplated his fate. Perhaps when they brought him out he could grab a rifle from one of the policemen and fight his way out of the execution yard. He had no fear of dying. He had lived with death for so long now it held no terror for him. His only regret was that he had not accomplished his mission.

He wondered what had happened to Miranda Diaz. From what he had learned from Conchella, the stolen bride was probably living with Gomez in his mountain hideout.

The more he learned about Gomez the more he become aware of the brutal nature of the man. The callous manner in which he had gatecrashed the wedding and treated everyone with brutal disregard set the measure of his vindictiveness.

That he had used the excuse of jealous revenge against Emile did not fool Hammer. Gomez had wanted the gold that he claimed Emile had stolen from him when he had run off with the woman Conchita. Whether Emile had been telling the truth, in that Conchita had absconded with the gold after enlisting Emile to help her, was a debatable point. Gomez hungered for gold and Hammer surmised that that was what drove the bandit.

The ruthless methods he employed to obtain the wealth were incidental. That cruel nature was only a weapon used to induce fear in his opponents and allies alike. That much was obvious in the reaction of the police chief when Gomez's lieutenant had ordered his execution. The captain had complied without question. His discomfiture was obvious when Hammer had queried his position.

The door to the outer rooms opened, interrupting any further speculation. Half a dozen young recruits filed inside. All were armed with carbines and Hammer guessed they were to be the firing squad. The captain followed.

'Manacles!' he barked.

His cell door was opened and with half a dozen weapons pointed into the cell Hammer submitted to being handcuffed. His arms were drawn behind and fastened, effectively dampening any hope of grabbing a weapon and making a last stand.

'Where is Father Dominick?' he asked.

The captain shrugged. 'I sent word last night but he has not turned up. I cannot delay any longer. I have many other duties to perform.'

'Has Gomez sent you his orders for the day?' Hammer said sarcastically.

The captain chose to ignore the jibe. He nodded curtly to his men and Hammer was escorted from the cell and marched outside.

Quite a crowd had gathered for the execution. Mothers with children mingled with saloon girls and *vaqueros*. They watched curiously as Hammer was escorted to the killing ground. This was simply a row of posts in front of an adobe wall. Numerous bullets had left the wall pockmarked as if by the activities of some mysterious boring insects. There was a stirring amongst the crowd of onlookers. Some parents lifted children up so they could obtain a better view.

Hammer was fastened to one of the uprights. The police captain stepped forward and faced the crowd.

'This man has been found guilty of murder. He murdered Conchella, a former friend of Gomez, and her brother Gabino. When we went to arrest him he shot down some of your policemen. For these crimes he will be executed. You are all called to witness that punishment.'

For Hammer the use of the name Gomez by the captain when making the proclamation was a significant reminder of the power the bandit chief wielded in these parts. The captain walked up to his prisoner. In his hand he held a scarf.

'Blindfold?' he asked.

Hammer shook his head.

'Do you have any last requests?'

'I would have liked a priest, but seeing that has been denied me I would like a cigar.'

Hammer had not smoked during his stay in San Cristobel but suddenly the craving for tobacco became overwhelming.

'I think that will be in order.'

The police chief produced a thin cigar and inserted it into the prisoner's mouth. He struck a match and Hammer sucked at the acrid smoke. It made him cough but he held the cigar between his teeth and sucked greedily. He felt slightly dizzy after so long an abstinence but he persevered. If he was going to die it made little difference if he felt some nausea as the bullets tore into his body.

By now the firing squad had been lined up. Half a dozen nervous recruits stared at him without malice. He had killed their companions but they were alive and it was a sunny morning. Tonight they would drink tequila and vie for the affections of the girls at the cantina. The American would die and life would go on as usual. A sergeant shouted out a command and the men came to attention.

'Aim!'

The carbines were levelled. Hammer lifted his gaze to the sky. It was a cloudless day and already the sun was hot. For some unaccountable reason the face of Anna Diaz surfaced in his mind.

He smiled as he remembered the expression on her face when he had kissed her. It would be good to bring her sister back. It would have been interesting to see her reaction to that. He waited for the bullets and hoped it would be a quick and clean death. He could hear someone shouting but he took no interest.

I should be reliving my life, he thought. It was said when death was imminent a person's life flashed before them. All he could think of was Anna Diaz and the anger in her as he grabbed her and kissed her. I bet no one ever did that to her before, he thought and laughed out loud.

'Señor Hammer, this is no laughing matter.'

He blinked and stared in bewilderment at the man standing before him. He was dressed in the garb of a Franciscan monk. Behind the monk, looking annoyed, was the police captain.

'Father Dominick,' he croaked. 'What are you doing here?'

'You asked for me, remember. I have come to help you make a good death.'

'You'll have to be quick, Father,' the

captain said impatiently. 'We need to get this over with.'

Father Dominick turned to the policeman. 'When it is your turn to die I don't suppose you will be in such a hurry. When a man goes to his maker he needs to know he is going to a benevolent God. If you give me some privacy, I will hear his confession and give him the last rites.'

Without replying the captain turned and strode away. The priest unfolded his stole and donned it.

'Now my son, would you like to make your confession?'

Ten minutes later the monk was still muttering prayers. Hammer had lost count of the times his confessor had raised his hands in blessings. In spite of his impending fate he could not rid himself of the image of Anna Diaz as he released her after kissing her full ripe lips.

He toyed with the idea of asking Father Dominick to send a message to the girl. Manuel could carry back his final communication. And then he wondered what had happened to the former *mayordomo*. He had left his travelling companion back at the Templo de la Cruz monastery. As he was about to ask Father Dominick about Manuel he saw a shadow looming behind the monk.

'Father!' The voice of the police captain was filled with suppressed irritation. 'Don't you think you have done enough to save this miserable murderer's soul?'

Father Dominick was of slight build. He turned to the policeman and seemed to swell in size as he glared in righteous indignation at the man who dared interrupt the work of God.

'Captain, I am a priest. I have been trained by the Church to carry out the holy rituals. Would I presume to tell you how to go about your duties? Could I instruct you in the business of catching criminals? Every man to his trade. Each to his own skills!'

The police captain's face grew red as

he tried to suppress his annoyance.

'I order you to move out of the line of fire immediately. If you do not move now I shall order my men to forcibly remove you. In which case I may well be obliged to charge you with obstructing police work.'

'I am a man of peace, Captain . . . '

He got no further. The captain half turned and motioned with his hand. Two young policemen strode forward and stood one each side of the priest.

'Do you walk under your own steam, Father, or shall you be carried from here?'

For a few moments the two men had an eyeball-to-eyeball confrontation. The policeman won. As he was hustled away the priest cast a last glance over his shoulder at the prisoner.

'Have courage my son. God is merciful.'

The rifles were lined up once more.

'Ready!'

A faint vibration in the ground, as if a herd of cattle or horses were thundering into the town, was discernible. Hammer could feel the tremor through his boots.

I wonder if they will bury me with my boots on, he speculated.

'Aim!'

He spat out the half-burnt cigar.

'Goodbye old world. No regrets.'

He stared up at the blue sky and waited for the blast from rifles that would be the last sound he would hear.

Which would come first, he wondered idly, the impact of the bullets or the detonation of the rifles. The herd of horses seemed very close.

The shots rang out. In spite of his resolution he flinched.

24

There was no pain. He brought his gaze down from the cerulean sky and blinked in surprise. The square was filled with horsemen. One kneed his mount towards him.

'Manuel!'

'Señor Hammer, I see we were in time. When the *rurales* came for Father Dominick I went out to find the army. I told the good father to try and delay the execution. I was fortunate to come across Captain Calleja last night. I had already made his acquaintance back at the Diaz ranch. It was lucky for you also he came so quickly.'

Hammer looked past Manuel and saw the soldiers. The firing squad was stranded within a circle of horsemen. The police captain was remonstrating with an officer in an ornate uniform. The officer held a smoking pistol in his hand. He was gesticulating with the weapon as he spoke. The soldiers had their carbines unlimbered and were pointing their weapons at the policemen. The firing squad had lowered their rifles and now glared sullenly at cavalrymen. With a contemptuous flick of his revolver the cavalry officer dismissed the police captain. He turned his horse around and rode over beside Manuel.

'Padre!' Captain Calleja said, 'you have put me to a lot of trouble. I just hope you will be grateful and return to your monastery.' He nodded to Manuel. 'Take him to the barracks. I'll have the police release him from those handcuffs.'

Some time later within the police headquarters Hammer was checking his possessions. He buckled on his revolver.

'The bag of money Don Eugene gave me is missing.'

Captain Calleja was seated behind the police captain's desk. A soldier was standing behind him, carefully brushing the dust of travel from his superior's ornate uniform.

'Captain Peralta, stealing from prisoners is a serious matter. If you return all his goods pronto, I may be willing to erase the charge of theft from your list of crimes. Already you are accused of the attempted execution of a prisoner without a trial and consorting with known bandits. I need not tell you of the seriousness of these misdemeanours.'

The police captain scowled at the army man but made no reply. Calleja sighed.

'What about his horse, or shall I add horse-stealing to the list of crimes?'

It was too much for the policeman. The army captain had taunted him right from the beginning. He was clearly exasperated by the interference of the army.

'I've no idea what happened to the murderer's horse,' he said tightly. 'I have twenty men under my jurisdiction. I can't be held responsible for their actions. They are paid very poorly and some might be tempted to steal from prisoners. I personally have never found any evidence of this. I don't even know if the condemned man owned a horse.'

'A superior officer is always responsible for his men's actions. My own men know the rules. I enforce them strictly. Private Lorenzo, tell the captain the four rules.'

The soldier brushing at the captain's uniform snapped to attention.

'A soldier must not steal unless it is to save his own life or the life of a comrade. His horse is cared for before his own comfort. He fights like he was fighting for his life. He never drinks while on duty.'

'And tell me, Lorenzo, what happens if my soldiers break any of these rules?'

'The punishment for breaking any of the four rules is twenty lashes for each infringement.'

'Discipline, my good captain.' Calleja waggled a forefinger at the police chief. 'Discipline is the key word. That is what is lacking in your department. Now to even more serious matters. Señor Hammer informs me an associate of Gomez Farias, one Mariano, walked into this police office and instructed you to execute your prisoner.'

'He is lying. Would you take the word of a gringo murderer against the chief of police?'

Calleja pursed his lips thoughtfully. 'A good point, Captain. So if this Mariano did not order the prisoner's execution then you must have held a trial. No policeman can condemn a man to death without a trial. Let me see the record of this trial.'

'I had no time for paperwork.' The police captain answered glibly. 'This man was too dangerous to be allowed to roam free. He had already killed three of my men. Perhaps I acted in haste and I regret this now.' Peralta shrugged. 'We all make mistakes.'

'Very well, Captain. There will have to be an inquiry into these matters. In the meantime you are relieved of your duties. My sergeant will take over the day to day running of the barracks. You will not leave El Ventio.'

He sat staring stonily at the police captain who rose to his feet, saluted stiffly and left the office. At last the captain turned his attention to the man at the centre of this fiasco. He stared critically at Hammer.

'I see you have armed yourself, Padre. I had hoped you would go back to your monastery and meditate on a beneficent God who allows vicious scum like Gomez Farias to roam free. Gomez is one of God's creations. Surely then God is ultimately responsible for the suffering Gomez inflicts on the rest of us?'

'Captain Calleja, God has given us all the gift of free will. How we use that freedom is down to us. A man or woman can choose the path of evil over the path of good.

'However I am not here to discuss good and evil. Also I am not a priest. I spent six months at San Christobel as a lay brother. At no time did I aspire to become an ordained priest. When Gomez hit that wedding party, among the several that were killed that day was a harmless old man. He was a friend of mine. I tried to stop Gomez on that day. It is to my eternal regret that I failed. I realized then that I was not fitted to a life of holy isolation so I buckled on this gun and I aim to rectify my failure to revenge that old priest. So don't call me padre again. My name is Joe Hammer.' He grinned without humour. 'Yes, I am still God's instrument but I sit no more in a monastery. With God's help I will smite those that offend Him. I am the Hammer of God.'

'The Hammer of God,' Calleja mused. He leaned forward and stared hard at the man opposite. 'Listen to me, hammer of whatever the hell you want to be, but bear in mind the next time you are in trouble I will not rush to rescue you. The only reason you are alive right now is because Manuel told me you were a friend of

Don Eugene. I have a mission to complete and no unfrocked priest will stand in my way of achieving that mission.'

'Good! We understand each other. I too am on a mission. I intend to find Gomez and I intend to make him pay for the death of one old priest. He's gonna realize that was one death too far. When I have killed Gomez, I shall try to rescue Señorita Miranda Diaz. I owe you, Calleja. You saved my life. If our paths cross again I shall remember that. But nothing will stand in my way when I go for Gomez.'

'Manuel, take this holy hammer out of my sight,' Calleja gritted out. 'Just remember I won't rescue the fool twice. If you both take my advice you will ride back to Don Eugene and tell him I am doing everything to rescue his daughter in spite of distractions from foreign fools.'

For a few poignant moments the two men stared at each other. There was an air of hostility and tension between them. At last Hammer tipped his hat, turned and stalked from the room. Manuel shrugged apologetically at the captain and followed.

25

The cantina was bustling as men drank and gossiped. Most of the tables were full and a few card games were in progress. Hammer had found a small table, hard against a wall, where he sat morosely regarding the drinkers. Manuel arrived with brimming glasses of beer and sat opposite him.

'What now, Señor Hammer?'

'For a start stop calling me Señor Hammer. Just call me Joe.'

'Joe.' The Mexican tried out the name and nodded. 'What now, Joe?'

'I came into El Ventio yesterday with the intention of getting a lead on Gomez.'

Hammer paused a moment as he wondered that so much had happened to him in such a short time. Conchella and her brother were dead, as were four policemen. He had stood in front of a firing squad and had been given the last rites. Then had come rescue when Manuel had brought Captain Calleja and his squadron of Mexican cavalry. All in twenty-four hours. He shook his head in exasperation.

'All I achieved was to get a young woman and her brother killed,' he went on. 'I thought that through them I would get a lead on Gomez. Now both are dead and I've no idea where to go next.'

Manuel nodded in sympathy. 'After we parted yesterday I left the convent and took a ride out. Talked to farmers and ranchers and *vaqueros*. As soon as I mention Gomez they become cagey. They talk about the weather or the sheep or cattle or horses but not about Gomez. Everyone is scared of him. He is like a pestilence afflicting this land. The only good thing that came out of my wanderings was the whereabouts of Captain Calleja so that I was able to find him and bring him back to save you.'

As Hammer nodded encouragingly Manuel took a long draught of his beer before continuing:

'What I did find out was that the *rurales* provided the captain with a guide. The only guiding he done was to lead Calleja and his soldiers around in circles. This Gomez is wily like a coyote, or should I say a wolf, for he terrorizes people into helping him. Those he can't frighten he bribes. Also, as we know, the local police are on Gomez's payroll.'

'Manuel, don't turn round, but Captain Peralta has just walked in. He's talking to a fella by the door.'

'Peralta, the police captain!' Manuel watched Hammer intently. 'What are you thinking, *amigo*?'

'I'm thinking the captain just might be wanting to send word to Gomez. Go quickly and get our horses ready. Unless I'm mistaken this fella might just lead us to Gomez.'

★ ★ ★

The messenger, if that was what he was, kept his pace to an easy jog. Hammer and his companion rode well behind trusting to following the sounds of the man ahead and their tracking skills to keep them in contact.

'Joe, if we keep this far behind, out of sight, it is possible we may lose him,' Manuel observed.

'It's a chance we have to take. Just leave this business to me. I've trailed enough men in the past. Believe me, if we get too close he'll be on to us. We'll get a fair idea what direction he's heading and if we do lose him we should be able to pick up the trail again. If the worst happens and he does give us the slip we'll lie in wait and nab him on the way back.'

They had come to a river and were riding along the bank. Both men were listening for the splash of a horse entering the water but so far the rider ahead was keeping on their side of the river. Even so, Hammer was keeping an eye on the ground, watching for signs of any deviation from the river bank. He pulled up sharply as he saw tracks indicating the rider ahead had cut away at right angles. Their quarry had turned on to a faint trail that had been beaten through the thick brush. Hammer turned his mount to follow. They were still moving at an even pace, the man ahead obviously still unaware he was being followed. All seemed to be going well till the brush thinned out and they saw open ground ahead. Sand! They had reached desert.

'Damn,' Hammer swore.

They could see their quarry ahead of them out on the sand. Once they broke cover they would be in plain sight if the man happened to turn and look behind. They reined in and sat examining the terrain ahead. In the distance they could see, crouching low, a long chain of hills.

'That's where he's heading,' Hammer observed.

'Somewhere in those hills is where Gomez is holed up. I guess we'll have to wait till dark to ride across this patch of open ground. If Gomez is as wily as we know he is he'll have lookouts posted to watch for riders. He'll have ample warning to vamoose or set up an ambush.' He looked about him. 'We'll head back to the river and water the horses, then find a place to rest up till nightfall. Then we'll make our way across that patch of desert. Come morning we'll cast around for tracks. I'm guessing we should find a trail where horses have been passing in and out of that place.'

'*Sí*, it is already late afternoon. We will not have long to wait till nightfall.'

Joe Hammer grinned across at his companion. 'We can't make a move till after midnight. I aim to be hid in those hills before first light. If we go too early we'll maybe blunder around and be seen. No, we'll make camp and try to get some rest.'

They found a grassy clearing and made a makeshift camp. They still had a few supplies from when they had been travelling to El Ventio. Risking a fire, they ate tortilla and beans washed down with strong, sweet coffee. Hammer unrolled his bedroll, lay down and within minutes was asleep. His companion watched him for a while then he too spread his blankets and lay down to rest.

Nothing disturbed the two sleepers. They were well away from any track and hidden within the thick brush. Hammer slept peacefully, the trauma of the past few days already in the past. He had a natural internal clock and if nothing else disturbed him he would wake just before it was time to move over the desert and into the hills to confront whatever dangers lay in wait for them.

26

When they started out again it was dark with a dull, orange moon that gave an eerie radiance across the sandy terrain. There was something sinister about the moonlight that gave Hammer an uneasy feeling. He could not shake off his edgy mood.

Ever since I gave up the holy life I been dogged by bad luck, he mused.

'God has abandoned me.'

'What was that, Joe?' Manuel queried.

'Huh!' Joe was not aware he had spoken aloud. 'Drop behind me. That way if I run into trouble you'll have a chance to hightail it outta danger. If that happens, go back to El Ventio and seek out Captain Calleja. He might just be able to take up from wherever you lose me.'

So they proceeded across the sand in

the direction of the hills.

Manuel was trailing about fifty yards in the rear. From time to time Hammer would look behind but could never be sure whether it was Manuel he could see or shadows that moved and appeared in the shape of a horseman.

He was aware of the change of sound as his horse began to tread more solid ground, an indication they were leaving the desert behind. The ground began to rise and he could make out the hills rising in front of him. He had turned around to see if Manuel was behind when the call came.

'Hey there, hey, *amigo!*'

Hammer stopped his horse, alert to any danger that might manifest itself.

'*Sí, compadre*, what is wanted?' he called.

'My horse she is gone lame. I think she threw a shoe. Now she has run off. Maybe you could help me round it up?'

'*Sí, amigo*, come over here and tell me where you last seen the animal.'

The voice had sounded from ahead

and slightly to the right. Hammer reached down and pulled his Colt.

'I am coming, *señor*.'

Hammer watched the shadowy figure emerge out of the shadows and was sure he saw the gleam of a weapon in the man's hand. He held his Colt with the barrel resting on his thigh, alert and watchful.

'*Gracias, señor*, I thought I would be marooned out here. No one ever comes this way.'

The man lunged swiftly, gripping Hammer's coat and jerking hard. If he had not been ready for trouble Hammer would have been caught out and pulled to the ground. His foot was well planted in the stirrup and his Colt was in his hand. With one smooth movement he brought the weapon down on the stranger's head. At the same time a gun blasted from the side. Joe did not know where the bullet went. He bent over and allowed himself to fall on top of the man he had just hit. The man was moaning and struggled feebly underneath the weight of Joe when he landed on him. Joe hit him again with his gun and the man went still.

'Hilario!' a voice called out. 'Did you get him?'

'*Sí*,' Hammer answered, keeping his voice low in an effort to confuse the back-up.

His attempt obviously failed, for the gun blasted out again lighting up the night. It was the signal for Manuel to open up from somewhere to the rear. The *mayordomo* was good and was placing his shots close to the gunman's position, keeping up a constant rate of fire.

Joe scrambled to his feet and began running forward in an attempt to get ahead of the ambusher. He was hoping Manuel would keep up his firing and distract the gunman from tracking his own movements. The strategy worked and the ambusher was engrossed in returning Manuel's fire.

Hammer could plainly see the flashes produced by the two guns now duelling it out. When he was far enough ahead he turned, raised himself cautiously to a crouching position and began to stalk the gunman.

He crept closer and closer to the man's position, expecting any moment the ambusher would realize what was happening and turn his weapon on this new threat. Then he saw the man plainly illuminated against the muzzle flash of his weapon. Joe steadied himself and waited. At the gunman's next shot he fired at the shadowy shape outlined in the gun flash.

Once, twice, three times he fired. The man rose up from his firing position. He had been kneeling behind a few boulders. He was trying to bring his rifle round to bear on Joe. Then Manuel got the man in his sights. He fired and the man was punched sideways as the heavy slugs hit him. There was a scream and a clatter as his weapon dropped from nerveless hands. The dark figure of the shooter disappeared from sight. Joe flattened himself to the ground in case the man was still dangerous, and waited. In the ensuing silence Manuel called out.

'Joe, you all right?'

'Sure thing. I think between us we managed to finish him.'

He went forward warily, his Colt held ready to fire if there was any movement from the downed man. He crouched beside the still figure and pushed his gun against the body as he found the neck and felt for a pulse.

'This one's a gonner,' he called. 'There's another one over there with a sore head.'

He turned and walked back towards the place where he had first encountered the ambushers. A low groan told him his attacker was still groggy.

'Up here, Manuel. They're both down.'

He waited for his companion to arrive. Manuel was leading his horse.

'Good work, Manuel. Where'd you learn to shoot like that?'

'I was not always a *vaquero*. As a

young man I spent some time as a corporal in the army.'

'Maybe we can induce this fella to tell us where Gomez's hideout is.'

His victim was sitting up. Hammer bent over and poked the barrel of his Colt into the man's face.

'I don't know why you attacked us, *amigo*. We were coming to find Gomez. We have important information about the movements of the troops searching for him. Will you take us to him?'

'You can go roast in hell! Gomez knows all about the soldiers. They are fools and are no threat to our great leader. He is familiar with their every comings and goings.'

Hammer sighed. 'I guess we'll havta do this the hard way. I'll shoot bits off you till you tell me what I wanna know.'

There was no response from the man. Hammer cocked his pistol.

'Joe,' Manuel whispered urgently. 'Listen.'

Hammer raised his head and stared

into the darkness. From out of the night came the sound of many horses along with the creak of saddle leather and the slight clinking of spurs and harness.

27

Hammer sat back on his heels and stared into the darkness. Gradually, as his eyes adjusted, he could make out the shadowy forms of silent horsemen. He cast his eyes around and surmised they were entirely surrounded.

'Jeez, what have we called down upon us?' he murmured.

Slowly he stood up, all thoughts of questioning his prisoner disappearing with this new development.

'You are entirely surrounded. Throw down all weapons. Stand up with hands raised above your heads. Failure to carry out these orders will bring about instant death.'

'Joe, what do we do?' queried Manuel.

'We do just as the man says,' Joe answered.

He tossed his Colt to the ground and

raised his hands high in the air.

'We're peaceful travellers,' he called. 'We were riding through and these fellas attacked us. We were just protecting ourselves.'

There came the sound of someone urging a horse forward and a horseman advanced till he was a few yards from the little group.

'Señor Hammer of God!' The disgust in the voice of Captain Calleja came over plainly. 'You are like a bad smell I can't get rid of.'

'Captain Calleja,' Hammer asserted with some relief. He started to lower his arms.

'Keep your hands in the air,' the captain snapped, then rattled out a barrage of orders to his men.

A group of soldiers came out of the darkness and approached. They hauled the injured bandit to his feet. Using their carbines they prodded the three men towards the captain.

'What are you doing out here, Señor Hammer of God?'

The captain managed to make Joe's nickname sound like an insult.

'We were following up a lead when these fellas jumped us. My guess is they're outlooks for Gomez. We managed to down one and capture this one. I was just about to question him when you showed up.'

'Seems somewhat suspicious you being out here. Were you riding to warn Gomez we were in the vicinity?'

'Hell, Captain,' Hammer exploded. 'We're both on the same side. Can't you see I want Gomez as much as you do?'

Ignoring Hammer's outburst, the captain leaned towards the bandit. 'Are you part of the vile band of men led by the devil Gomez?'

'No, General, my horse had gone lame and I asked these bandits for help. They attacked us without provocation. I hear them boasting they killed my friend.' The man crossed himself. 'May God have mercy on his soul.'

Risking Calleja's wrath Hammer

lurched forward and punched the man on the side of the head.

'You lying dog,' he gritted as the bandit staggered back. 'You tell us where Gomez hangs out or I beat you to a pulp.'

Hammer stood with his fists clenched ready to do as he threatened.

'Help me, General,' the man pleaded. 'I have no idea what this madman is talking about.'

'Restrain that man!' Calleja snapped out.

Two soldiers grabbed Hammer and pulled him back from his victim.

'Goddamn it, Captain,' Hammer raged, 'you know I'm telling the truth. He's our only lead. I'll get the truth outta him if you'll let me.'

'Put him in irons,' Calleja ordered. 'Some of you men get a fire going. We're stopping here for a short while — at least till daybreak.'

'Hell, you can't do this!' Hammer protested as the men holding him fastened cuffs on his wrists. 'I'm an

American citizen. When this gets out how you treated me you'll have a war on your hands.'

Captain Calleja's laugh was of genuine amusement. 'Perhaps you are a spy for the American Government, Señor Hammer of God. When we first meet you are posing as a priest. Then I find you attacking and killing the *rurales* in El Ventio. Now you are out here attempting to contact Gomez. My guess is that you are an agent of the Americans and have come here to recruit Gomez to your cause. You will use him to ferment trouble for us so we are distracted from the real threat, which is the greedy Americans trying to take over more of our country. Perhaps Captain Peralta had the right idea when he put you in front of a firing squad.'

Hammer was staring in disbelief at the cavalry officer. 'You can't really believe all that bullshit. I want Gomez because he killed a friend of mine. I aim to make him pay for all the misery and pain he caused that day in San

Christobel. So if you just release me and give me back my guns and my horse and my captive I'll just forget all the indignities you are piling on me.'

While this conversation was going on there was buzz of activity around them as the soldiers dismounted and set up camp. A fire was being kindled nearby.

'Bring the American and his friend.'

The captain strolled over to the fire and stood before the flames. He was rattling out instructions to his troops. Hammer and Manuel were hustled to the fire. Pans of water were being heated and soon the rich aroma of brewed coffee drifted into the night.

'Damn you, Captain,' Hammer snarled, his anger mounting. 'Your superior will hear of this. When I get back I'm writing a letter of complaint.'

'Ah,' Calleja mused. 'That would be an interesting situation. The letter wouldn't do you much good if you were shot as a spy.'

'You know damn well I'm no spy!' Hammer raged. 'Who the hell am I supposed to be spying for? Our government has no interest in this miserable, dried-up, impoverished latrine you call a country.'

'Dear me, Señor Hammer of God,' Calleja said mildly. 'You are becoming quite abusive and tiresome. What sort of God is it that uses foulmouthed brutes posing as priests for his work? Though I suppose being a hammer you have to be both blunt and brutal. I think Hammer of Beelzebub would be a more appropriate name for you.'

'Give me the name of your superior.' Hammer was almost impotent with rage and could see no way of getting through to his tormentor. 'I'll see you broken for this. No one can treat foreign nationals like this with impunity.'

'By all means you can have the name of my superior. My uncle General Bargas is always keen to hear of my exploits. He will be most interested to receive your complaints. He might even promote me for capturing an American spy. He has every reason to hate the Americans. He lost an arm at Almoast. I will have pen and paper put at your disposal.'

Before Hammer could think up a suitable reply the scream came ululating out of the darkness. It was the scream of a man in mortal agony.

Hammer stared across at Captain Calleja but the captain did not seem bothered by the sounds of a man in terror for his life. He was just accepting a steaming mug from a soldier. Casually he sipped at the coffee and stared reflectively into the fire. The shriek of terror came again and Hammer shivered.

'Goddamn it, Captain, what the hell's going on?'

28

The soldier came strolling out of the darkness and into the flickering light of the fire. He saluted Captain Calleja.

'He talked?' the captain asked.

'*Sí, Capitán.*'

The soldier had a broad flat face with thin cruel lips. Hammer figured he was full-blooded Indian.

'There is a small valley a mile or so back in the hills. The way into it is through a narrow ravine. Men with rifles are posted along the rim and can pour down much lead on anyone coming through the ravine.'

'Take two men and go check it out. Be careful not to be seen. But I'm sure Gomez knows we are here. That gun battle with his lookouts must have alerted him. Did he say whether there was a back way out?'

The soldier shook his head. 'He says

not. But Gomez is a wily *lobo*. It would not be his way to allow himself to be trapped in a blind.'

'I think you are right. Good work. Come back quickly with your report.'

The soldier saluted and Hammer watched him walk out into the night.

'Perhaps you believe me now that I was telling the truth and free me from these shackles,' he asked the captain, holding out his manacled wrists.

'On the contrary, Señor Hammer of God, I want you where I know you are out from under my feet. In the last few days you have put me to a lot of bother. I had to break off my patrols to ride to your rescue. No, Hammer of God, you and your friend will stay here under guard while I go hunt this wily Gomez.'

'Damn you, Calleja, release me at once!' Hammer raged.

The captain ignored him and was issuing a stream of orders. The soldiers were soon ready to move out. The unconscious bandit was carried in and handcuffed. The man's shirt was ripped and Hammer could see dark patches of blood weeping from his eyes and nostrils. Calleja left two soldiers to guard the prisoners and Hammer could only watch helplessly as the rest of the company moved out. He sat by the fire and stared morosely after the departing men.

Dawn had still not arrived when they heard the horses again. The soldiers who guarded them had been taking turns to doze. Now they suddenly stood to attention.

'Halt, who goes there!'

There was no reply. The men fumbled their carbines ready and stared nervously out into the darkness. Again they called out a challenge, aiming their weapons out into the night. This time they did get an answer. Guns suddenly flamed, lighting up the murky darkness.

Hammer had been crouching a few yards from the fire, whispering to Manuel as they discussed ways and means of effecting their escape. He threw himself flat when the firing broke out. Their guards stood no chance as a hail of bullets swept into the campsite. They staggered back as the bullets thudded home, punching holes in shabby uniforms. So sudden and unexpected was the barrage neither of the men managed to return fire. They fell like boneless puppets. The thread that controlled their lives suddenly severed — they were already dead before they hit the earth.

Hammer lay hugging the ground as the crackle of gunfire slowly diminished. Someone shouted an order and the firing subsided. The horses came on in. Hammer lay where he was watching the riders.

'See if any are still alive,' a voice ordered.

Men were dismounting and moving to the fire. Hammer sat up, his hands raised high above his head. He did not speak for he was fairly certain as to the identity of the raiders. As the raiders saw him guns were pointed in his direction.

'Don't shoot. We're handcuffed. We have no weapons.'

Both he and Manuel were surrounded and hauled to their feet.

'It is true. They are shackled.'

One of the riders dismounted and walked over to the prisoners. Hammer stared at the man. It was as he suspected. This was the man Captain Calleja and his soldiers had set out to entrap in his lair, Gomez Farias. Before he could speak someone called out.

'Gomez, it is Hilario. He has been beaten.'

The bandit chief turned from Hammer towards the voice. Since he had been dragged back to the fire Hilario had not stirred. Now he groaned as he was hauled to his feet.

'Gomez,' he gasped as he recognized the man before him. 'The soldiers tortured me but I would not tell them anything.'

'You are a brave man, Hilario. The soldiers must have guessed the location of my hideout. Even now they are attacking the place where I was. How did they guess all that? But you did not tell them.'

'*Sí, sí.*' The man was nodding vigorously. 'I would never betray you.'

'You are a good and loyal follower. I am going to reward you. Are you in much pain?'

'Gomez, the pain it is terrible. Those soldiers are animals. I will show you what they did to me and yet I would not tell them anything.'

'No!' Gomez held up a hand. 'Do not show me. My delicate nature would not stand such horrors. Here, this is for the pain.'

Gomez took out his pistol and cocked it. Hilario shrank back.

'No, I told them nothing . . . please . . . '

Gomez put the gun to the man's forehead. The gunshot cut his protests short. His head jerked back as the heavy slug ploughed through. A spray of brain and blood exploded from the back of his skull. The men holding him released the dead man and jumped quickly away. Gomez stood staring down at the body.

'Nobody betrays Gomez Farias,' he said and turned back to the two prisoners. 'Who are you?'

'We heard about the army searching for you and were riding to warn you,' Hammer said hastily. 'They caught us and were holding us. We stood no chance against so many.'

The bandit stood observing Hammer and Manuel, all the time toying with his gun. Before he could react to this piece of information there was the movement of horses behind him. He turned and watched as three riders approached. Hammer peered at the trio. One was a young woman. Two heavily armed bandits flanked her.

'Ah, Miranda, my dear, do you want a warm before we carry on into El Ventio? Captain Calleja was thoughtful enough to provide us with this splendid campsite.'

There was no response from the girl. She sat slumped in the saddle.

'No? Then we will proceed to town.' Gomez walked towards his horse and swung aboard. 'Bring them,' he ordered, pointing to Hammer and Manuel. Wheeling his horse he cantered out from the camp.

Manuel and Hammer were hustled towards their mounts. In moments the two captives were in the centre of the bandit gang as they rode out into the desert towards El Ventio. In his hurry and in the dim light Gomez had not recognized Hammer. Once the bandit was in El Ventio, when he had more leisure to question him, Hammer felt sure he could expect the same end as had befallen the ill-fated Hilario.

29

Hammer guided his horse close to Manuel.

'I'm going to make a break when we get to the river,' he hissed. 'We won't stand a chance once we get to town. Captain Peralta will soon put Gomez right about us. When I go they'll be so busy trying to bring me down it'll give you a chance as well.'

'He has Señorita Diaz with him. What about her?'

'We won't be able to help her if we're dead or locked in Peralta's prison with a firing squad booked for the morning. That is if Gomez doesn't finish us off himself.'

'*Sí*, I will be ready. God go with you. If we are successful where shall we meet up again?'

'You recall that place we camped last night? We'll meet there.'

There was a sudden movement beside him and a rifle stock whacked Hammer across the shoulders. The blow was unexpected and painful.

'Quiet!' hissed the bandit who had been assigned to guard the prisoners. 'If you are plotting an escape I can tell you I am a very good shot with this rifle.'

Again the weapon thudded into Hammer.

'Goddamn it! That hurt!' he yelled.

With sudden anger he reached out with his manacled hands and grabbed at the weapon as the bandit was striking him again. More by chance than good aim his hands closed on the wooden stock. He jerked at the weapon and twisted viciously. The bandit screamed as his fingers were caught in the firing mechanism. The rifle went off and the bandit stopped screaming as the bullet ploughed into his stomach. He fell across the neck of his mount. The animal kicked out and bucked. It was enough to unseat the wounded man. He plunged to the ground.

Hammer slammed his heels into his mount's flanks. Already spooked by the plunging horse beside it and noise of the shot, the animal instantly took off into the night. Desperately Hammer tried to hold on to his seat and at the same time keep his grip on the rifle. Somehow he managed to do both. So sudden was the action that the bandits were caught out as their prisoner raced away into the night. There were a few shots fired but nothing came near Hammer.

He kept the horse going at a fast pace, for he knew Gomez would send men after him. That cautious old fox would leave nothing to chance and would want to recapture his prisoner if only to have the pleasure of killing him.

As he rode he kept listening for sounds of pursuit. Sure enough he could make out the faint pounding of hoofs somewhere to his rear. He would have to lose his pursuers or, failing that, make a stand.

What one lone man, manacled, and

armed with only a rifle could accomplish against Gomez's bandits was debatable. He would have to stand and fight or give up and be butchered. Hammer was cornered and at a severe disadvantage but he was going to put up a fierce resistance. If he did go down then the men who pursued him would pay a heavy price to achieve that.

Not knowing the territory and with only the rendezvous he had arranged with Manuel before his abortive breakaway, Hammer began to figure out his options. To give himself freer movement with his manacled hands he slid the rifle he had so deftly taken from the bandit into the saddle sheath. Taking a firmer grip on the reins he now had more control over the bolting horse.

Slowly he began to angle his horse towards the river. If he guessed right then he would be running on a parallel course to the main band of bandits. He knew they were heading for El Ventio. Gomez had said as much. Once he got to the river he would know where he was. But first he had to shake off the men on his tail.

On they rode and Hammer began to make out features in the area he was passing through. He realized dawn was not far off. As he rode he kept listening out for the men running behind him. Their horses seemed evenly matched and Hammer guessed the bandits were not gaining on him. He had no illusions about the men pursuing him. They would most likely keep after him till they caught up with him or killed him with a lucky shot. He did not believe they would give up. Gomez ruled by fear. Their failure to capture or kill him would bring swift retribution from the brutal bandit leader.

Hammer had seen at first hand what happened to the men the bandit chief considered had failed him. They never got a second chance. The men pursuing him had no option. They would have to keep on after him. It boiled down to a simple choice for the hunters and the hunted. It was kill or be killed.

The growing daylight was now such that he could make out the line of trees in the distance marking out the course of the river. The dull reports of the rifle shots from behind made him realize that the dawn had brought him into view of the men chasing him. They were taking turns to fire and the steady reports of their rifles caused him to bend low over the neck of his mount and try to coax more speed from the animal.

Hampered as he was by his manacles it would be difficult for him to return fire. He had to endure and hope he got to the river before a stray bullet brought him down. It would be a close-run thing. And he was not sure what conditions he would meet at the river. Once in the shelter of the trees and bushes he might be able to make a stand. Then the bandits got lucky. The horse stumbled as the bullet punched into its hind leg.

Hammer felt the gait of the horse alter and the horse was slowing.

Hammer grabbed for the rifle butt and extracted it from the scabbard. He glanced behind. The bandits were still firing systematically. Then the horse stumbled and Hammer knew it was going down.

He pulled his boots from the stirrups and waited for the inevitable. Then the horse was on his knees and Hammer was rolling over the downed beast's head and desperately hanging on to the rifle — his only means of survival now that he had lost his mount.

30

With his hands shackled Hammer was finding it difficult to keep from being injured as he tumbled to the ground. He kept rolling forward, for he feared the wounded beast would fall on him. Bruised and breathless he swivelled on the ground and looked back. His horse was neighing shrilly with legs windmilling as it tried to stand on its injured leg. Hammer saw the leg twisted beneath its belly and the beast was writhing in agony as it squealed in pain.

Far out he saw the bandits still riding swiftly towards him. Risking a blow from those thrashing hoofs he crawled quickly to the head of the wounded animal. With a quick motion he jammed the muzzle of his rifle into the soft jaw of the horse and quickly pulled the trigger. The explosion jolted the horse's head as the bullet entered its brain. With a few spasmodic twitches the beast subsided. Quickly Hammer threw himself behind the belly of the dead animal and took aim at the bandits riding to finish him.

'Steady,' he murmured as he centred on one of the horsemen.

The rifle jacked against his shoulder and the leading rider was suddenly thrown back as the rifle slug hit him in the chest. He catapulted over the rump of his mount and hit the ground bumping and rolling with the momentum till his lifeless body came to a stop. His mount carried on running.

Hammer switched to the man in the centre. The remaining three were wheeling their mounts to ride either side of their downed quarry. Hammer aimed again — squeezed off his shot. His dead horse made an ideal shooting platform. A second man toppled from his horse. Bullets were hitting into the carcass of Hammer's mount as the remaining two bandits sought to finish him. Hammer ignored the incoming lead and coolly took aim for a third shot.

He shot too low this time and hit the horse. The animal screamed as the bullet ploughed through its chest and ruptured a lung. Then it was on its knees and the rider was thrown over its head in much the same manner as was Hammer when he came off, only Hammer, expecting his horse to collapse, had managed to roll into the fall without too much damage. The bandit was not so fortunate. He catapulted over the horse's head and smashed into the ground. His horse, valiantly trying to go on, plunged across the man's body and the bandit's screams were cut off abruptly.

Then Hammer was desperately throwing himself to one side as the last bandit leapfrogged his bunker and was firing his rifle down at him as his horse sailed over. Then he was past and Hammer stood up. Deliberately he took aim and fired rapid shots into the back of the bandit as he was hauling on the reins to come back for another run. The man arched upwards as the bullets cut into him. Then he too was tumbling into the dirt.

Hammer sat down on his dead horse and watched for movement from his four victims. The only movement he could detect were the horses wandering aimlessly now that their masters had gone.

Out on the sands the wounded horse was squealing piteously as it stood with head down and blood pouring from mouth and nostrils. Wearily Hammer stood and walked over to the wounded beast. For the second time that night he put a bullet in a horse's brain.

'I only wish it were Gomez I was finishing off,' he said regretfully to the horse as he placed the rifle against its ear.

Slowly he made a circuit of the downed bandits. All were dead. As he came to each one he searched them for weapons and ended up with a stiletto and a pair of ebony-handled Colts. He took what ammunition he could carry. One of the men had a canteen and when he uncorked it he smelled the rich aroma of alcohol.

'Wow,' he gasped as he took a long draught of the liquor. 'I sure as hell needed that.' Moodily he stared at his shackles. 'I sure could do with losing these.'

The shackles were made up of two bars joined in the centre with a jointed link and attached to the metal bands that encircled his wrists. Thoughtfully he took one of the Colts and weighed it in his hand. With some effort he wedged the weapon underneath the saddle of his dead mount. He attached a piece of rawhide to the trigger and placed the end in his mouth.

'All I stand to loose is a hand,' he muttered fatalistically as he wedged the centre link of the shackles in the muzzle of the captive Colt. 'Here goes nothing.'

He tugged at the rawhide. The Colt blasted out and he felt the shackles dig painfully into his wrists. There was a feeling of elation as the link disintegrated and his hands were free. The wristbands were still in place and the metal bars that had been joined by the central link now dangled loosely. He recovered the Colt, took the gunbelt he had recovered from a dead bandit and strapped that on. His next task was to capture a horse.

He had trouble stalking the frightened beasts. The ponies were skittish, made nervous by the smell of blood in the morning air. At last his patient and soft approach paid off and he caught up with one horse. Once he was mounted the second horse was easily rounded up. For long speculative moments he looked out at the dead bandits before riding across to the nearest body.

With a lot of grunting effort he loaded the dead man across the saddle of one of the surviving horses. He removed the man's revolver from his holster and stuffed it inside the dead man's waistband. Then he pulled down the bandit's coat to hide the weapon.

He remounted and, leading the captured horse with its grisly burden and without a backward look, he headed in the general direction of the river.

'I just gotta make that rendezvous with Manuel, providing he managed to make a break for it.'

It took him some time to find the original camp where he and Manuel had spend the hours waiting to cross the desert. It was empty. Deciding to wait a while longer in case his missing companion turned up Hammer dismounted and secured his mounts to a large tree.

Squatting on the ground he laid out his array of armaments. Then he set to work cleaning and testing each weapon. When he had finished he holstered the twin Colts and returned the rifle to the saddle boot. As well as weapons he had looted a considerable amount of ammunition from the dead bandits. Lastly he pushed the stiletto into his boot top.

He thought of the odds stacked

against him in El Ventio and frowned up at the buttery sun, now riding high in the sky. His was a lonely situation. The town would be crawling with bandits and from all he had seen so far Captain Peralta and his policemen would be backing Gomez and his gang.

'If it is they will, God, let this humble instrument of yours carry out your designs.'

He bowed his head for a moment in silent prayer. Then abandoning any hope that Manuel was free to rejoin him he mounted up and began the ride into El Ventio.

31

As he had anticipated, the town was swarming with heavily armed men. Hammer rode boldly into the town. With so many strangers in the town he did not believe he would be challenged. Nevertheless a group of men in the street eyed him suspiciously as he rode up. A couple separated from the group and stepped into the roadway barring his progress.

'*Buenas tardes.*' Hammer spoke first, hoping to forestall any awkward questioning. 'Where can I find Gomez? I brought in the *hombre* that escaped. Thought he might wanna know what happened.'

The ploy worked. Squinting up at him the men took in his dusty clothing and the body slumped over the spare horse. They believed what Hammer wanted them to believe.

'You will find him up at Hotel San Felice.' The man pointed up the street.

'*Gracias.*'

Hammer nudged his mount forward. He could feel a tingle in the small of his back as he went beyond the little knot of men. Any moment he expected a challenge but none came and he let the horse amble at its own pace along the street. Mingled with his apprehension was a sense of the absurd as he wondered what Gomez would think when Hammer presented him with the body of one of his own men. That is if he ever got that far.

'Hotel San Felice,' he murmured as he spotted the sign.

More bandits stood around the entrance as Hammer pulled up and dismounted.

'This is the fella as escaped. Gomez sent me out after him. Give me a hand to carry him inside.'

They eyed him suspiciously.

'We guard the hotel. We don't carry dead bodies.'

Hammer looked startled. 'Goddamn it, he gone and died on me! Hell, I just hope the payout is for dead or alive.'

He struggled to get the body from the horse on to his shoulder and walked past the bemused guards. As he stepped inside a man was just walking to the door. He looked at Hammer and his mouth fell open.

'You!'

The man facing him was Mariano, Gomez's lieutenant. Hammer, not expecting to be recognized so soon, reacted quickly. With Herculean effort he heaved the body at the bandit. Mariano was going for his gun once he recognized Hammer. The body of his dead comrade crashed into him and hurtled him from his feet. Even as he went down the bandit had his gun unlimbered and let off a shot at Hammer.

Hammer had his own pistol in his hand. His bullet caught Mariano in the throat and ploughed up through his skull and out of the back of his head. As the two bodies sprawled on the carpet the men in the lobby were whirling around, startled by the gunshots. Hammer dropped to the floor where the bodies of Mariano and the dead bandit he had carried so patiently in from the desert gave him shelter of a kind.

The door behind him was opening as the guards posted outside pushed inside. He twisted round to meet the threat from the rear but was saved by the hail of bullets loosed by the men in the lobby as they fired at the intruder.

He kept his head low as lead swept the place where he had been standing seconds before. A man yelled out in pain and the door slammed shut as the guards quickly backed out again.

There was a lot of confused yelling from the men in the lobby. Hammer risked a look and fired a few rapid shots at the panicky men gathered by the large glass doors that led to the interior of the hotel. His bullet brought one man down cursing as the slug hit him in the side. Another bullet smashed the glass in the door.

At the noise of crashing glass from behind them the men cringed and threw startled glances over their shoulders. By now Hammer was on his knees with both revolvers out. He fired deliberately, picking his targets. Men were yelling in panic and two more went down with gunshot wounds. There was a concerted rush through the damaged doors as men fled from Hammer's deadly shots.

He fired into the backs of the fleeing bandits and saw two more men go down under his bullets. As his guns clicked on empty, he quickly holstered them. Knowing he had no time to reload he grabbed up the fallen pistol from the dead Mariano. He ran across the lobby and slid behind the large wooden desk to find a frightened woman cowering there.

'*Buenas tardes*,' Hammer greeted her. 'Keep flat on the floor and you'll be OK. Which room is Gomez in?'

'T . . . t . . . twenty t . . . t . . . three.'

Her teeth were chattering as she answered him. He saw the shotgun on the shelf.

'Can I borrow your little gun?' he asked as he slid the weapon out.

He was up and running for the doors before she could frame a reply. Through the broken doors he could see the men clustered on the other side. He let fly with both barrels of the borrowed gun.

'Eat lead!' he grunted as he crashed through the ruined doors.

Bandits were yelling and scrambling to get away. He did not see the bodies on the floor and he stumbled and went down. The fall saved his life as the men back in the street ventured inside once more and fired through the ruined doors at him. Additional damage tore into the fleeing bandits as the bullets swept over Hammer and dispatched a few more of them.

On all fours Hammer scrambled after the fleeing bandits. There were two avenues of escape — a corridor heading to the rear of the hotel and a broad carpeted stairway leading to the upper floor. The survivors of the onslaught were fleeing down the corridor.

Hammer chose to go up. At the foot of the stairway he paused long enough to fire a couple of shots back into the lobby at the men who had ventured inside. Then he mounted the stairs taking two at a time and tensed as he expected bullets from up ahead and from behind.

He flung himself flat on the landing. His breath coming in heaving gulps, he lay for a moment gathering his strength for his next move. He could hear confused shouting from below. Doors were slamming in the corridor ahead of him. Hoarse voices called out, demanding to know what was happening. He risked sticking his head around the corner at floor level. He was just in time to see someone disappear beyond the bottom corner. Otherwise the corridor was empty. He was instantly on his feet. Swiftly he strode along the carpeted hallway, scanning doors as he went.

'Number twenty-three,' he muttered as he spotted the room number.

He drew back, then kicked out viciously with his heel. The door crashed inwards as the lock broke under the kick. Then he was rolling inside, his gun in hand and not quite knowing what he was blundering into.

32

The room was empty, or so he thought. Then he saw the figure in the chair, unmoving — staring back at him. The features were distorted and bloody and yet he recognized the man.

'Manuel! What the . . . '

He was moving towards the *mayordomo*, his eyes alert for any of the bandit gang. Manuel seemed to be alone in the room. As he came further into the room he saw the ropes binding him to the chair.

'Don't worry, old buddy, we'll soon have you free.'

He extracted the stiletto from his boot top and moved to cut the bindings. Then he saw the finger ends, splayed out and bloody — the nails missing. There was blood also on Manuel's face and smeared blood around his mouth and chin.

Hammer's foot crunched on something and he looked down at the carpet. Small yellow pebbles! There was blood trailing from the pebbles and suddenly Hammer realized he was treading on teeth.

'Jeez!' he whispered as he bent and began slicing at the rope holding the *mayordomo* to the chair. 'What have they done to you, old friend?'

Hammer slid his arm under the man's shoulders and helped him across to the bed. Manuel slumped across the covers with faint whimpers of pain.

'Was it Gomez?'

'Miranda, she . . . she . . . let it out who I was.'

The words were gasped out giving glimpses of the bloodied devastation inside the man's mouth. Bloodstained saliva and clots of blood were disgorged with each movement of the lips.

'She . . . she's not to blame . . . she was just so pleased to see me. Gomez and Mariano did this. Wanted . . . to know who was with me. I . . . I told him about you.' The eyes pleaded for forgiveness.

'It's all right, old-timer. It makes no difference. Gomez and me, we have a score to settle. This only adds to the account.' Hammer looked helplessly down at the ruined man on the bed. 'I gotta go after him now. I . . . I'll come back for you. Take you home to Don Eugene. They'll look after you.'

'Joe.'

The hand came off the bed reaching towards him. Hammer hesitated — reached out and gently took the damaged hand in his.

'Joe, don't worry about me. Save Miranda. Take . . . take her back to her father.'

Joe stared down at his friend and the man began to choke as blood and mucus from his ruined mouth ran back into his throat.

'Joe . . . '

Manuel began coughing and choking on his own blood. Quickly Joe rolled him on his side. Dark globules spewed from his mouth and dribbled on to the pillow. While he worked with the injured man Hammer was listening to the noises around the hotel. There were shouts and doors slamming but no one approached the door of room twenty-three. He could hear no gunfire.

'They thought it was the soldiers come back,' Manuel finally gasped when he had recovered sufficiently to talk again. 'They'll come after you.'

Thoughtfully Hammer sat on the bed beside his wounded companion and began ejecting spent shells. When he finished pushing fresh shells into the chambers he now had three fully loaded pistols. He would give a good account of himself.

'Give me a gun, Joe.'

Hammer stared down at the man's damaged hands — the ends raw and weeping blood where the nails had been ripped out. He watched with horrified fascination as the ruined hand reached out. Hesitantly he placed the gun in the hand made slippery with the man's own blood.

Hammer stood up and walked to the window. Looking out he could see a sloping roof below. He opened the window and turned back to the bed. Manuel was crawling like an injured insect across the bed. Before he could come to the man's aid he had slipped off the bed on to the floor. Quickly Hammer came across to the bed as Manuel struggled to sit upright. The bloody hand still gripped the revolver.

'What . . . ?' Hammer asked.

The lips twitched in the parody of a grin as more blood dribbled from the ruined mouth.

'When they come through that door I shall have my revenge.'

Manuel placed his hand on top of the bed and lined up the barrel of the revolver with the broken door. Hammer reached out and placed a hand on Manuel's shoulder.

'*Adios, amigo*. We will meet again soon and you will teach me to drink tequila.'

They both knew there was very little likelihood of their meeting again. While Hammer's chances of surviving in a town full of hostile bandits and corrupt policemen all hunting for his scalp were slim, Manuel with his ruined hands had even less chance.

'Just save Miranda . . . '

Hammer nodded, gave a last squeeze on the wounded man's shoulder and turned to the window. Someone was shouting in the corridor outside the room. He slipped a leg over the windowsill and gave one last look at his companion.

Manuel was kneeling behind the bed with his forearms resting on the bed. His gun was trained on the doorway. He did not look to the window as Hammer slid outside and hung for a few moments before dropping the few feet to the roof.

It was easy — all . . . too . . . easy. They were waiting in the alleyway below.

'You make a move towards those

guns, Padre, and you will walk with the angels tonight.'

Hammer stared at the men at each end of the alleyway. There were at least a dozen guns levelled at him. Gomez stood with them.

Hammer stared at his enemy. His hands twitched but he knew he would be mown down in a hail of lead if he followed his instincts and pulled his Colts.

'So your friend was right. It was you. You sure are a strange priest. Bring him!'

Hammer's shoulders slumped in defeat. He held his hands well out from his sides. Then the shots blasted out from the room where he had left Manuel with a loaded revolver. His captors flinched and glanced up. It was instinctive. Only a deaf man could ignore the noise of battle taking place in that bedroom.

In one fluid movement Hammer turned and drew at the same time. Guns flaming, he ran towards the men blocking his escape route. Two of them reeled back as his shots struck home. Their companions saw Hammer coming towards them and began to fire their own weapons.

Hammer flung himself to the ground and even as he rolled he was still firing. Then he was in amongst them, his body cannoning into legs and bringing them down like skittles. In the confusion he clubbed out with his empty weapons, striking at the few men still able to fight back. Then he was on his feet and running the last few feet for the corner. A red-hot missile hit him a tremendous blow on the shoulder and he twisted round in agony. As he fell they were on him like coyotes on a wounded buffalo.

'Damn!' he muttered as the pain in his shoulder paralysed his arm. With so many attacking him it was impossible to fight back. They hauled him to his feet as Gomez arrived from the other end of the alleyway with the rest of the gang trailing after him.

As Hammer hung there, his arms

gripped by men on each side, Gomez put his pistol to the prisoner's head. Hammer was remembering Gomez doing exactly the same thing to one of his own men back at the desert camp. The shot had blown away the man's head. He stared stoically at the bandit.

'I should kill you now, Padre,' Gomez spat out, pushing so hard with his pistol that Hammer's head was forced back as the hard steel bored painfully into his forehead. 'But you would want to suffer just like your friend upstairs. Holy men are like that.'

33

They had to step over the dead men Hammer had slain in the lobby. Gomez stopped by one body and knelt down. It was his right-hand man, Mariano.

'I will make you suffer for this!' Gomez hissed.

More of Hammer's handiwork was sprawled in bloody disarray in the hallway leading to the stairs. Gomez eyed the bodies and looked speculatively at his prisoner.

'Did you do all this on your own?'

Hammer grinned through the pain.

'I had God behind me. *The Lord preserveth all them that love him: but the wicked he will destroy.*'

Another body was sprawled in the corridor outside the room where Hammer had found Manuel. Gomez could not contain his rage. In sudden passion he struck out at Hammer with his pistol, catching him on the temple. The blow was brutally hard and Hammer sagged to his knees and the men holding him had to drag him the last few paces to room twenty-three.

Inside the room another two bandits lay on the carpet leaking blood. They found Manuel sprawled behind the bed — his chest covered in blood. He had gone down fighting and had taken two of his opponents with him.

'Get him in the chair.'

Gomez was growing more and more incensed as the body count mounted. Hammer had to keep from crying out as his captors, ignoring his wounded shoulder, forced him into the chair that had held Manuel while he had been tortured.

'The pliers.'

Gomez held out his hand. His men gave each other worried looks then looked vaguely around the room.

'Pliers!' Gomez roared in sudden anger. He struck the man nearest him. 'Pliers!'

'Mariano!' a man exclaimed with sudden insight. 'Mariano always carried the pliers.'

In his anger and frustration Gomez began to kick and punch the men in the room.

'Go get them then!' he screamed. 'Mariano is lying downstairs. Killed by this so called holy man.'

Men scrambled to do his bidding. For the time being Hammer was left unattended as the bandits vied with each other to do their chief's bidding. He was slumped on the chair with his head drooping forward. His hand slid towards his boot and his fingers found the hilt of the stiletto. There was one man each side of Hammer. He slid out the stiletto and at the same time rose from the chair.

The blow was hard and sure — the slim blade entering under the man's chin. The stricken man staggered back and Hammer went with him groping for the bandit's holstered weapon. He could hear the man's companion cursing as he saw what was happening. Hammer was falling to the floor and the weapon was coming clear of the dying man's holster. Gomez had turned at the disturbance and fired wildly at the struggling men.

The man with Hammer's stiletto in his throat was dying anyway — the bullets from Gomez's gun finished him off. Hammer had used the dead bandit as a shield as they fell. He was trying to sight on the bandit chief with his stolen gun. He got one round off before the bandit chief dived for the door. The remaining men in the room were pushing to follow their leader. Hammer fired another round into the doorway and had the satisfaction of hearing someone scream. He could hear Gomez shouting instructions.

'Bring the Diaz woman!'

'Damn!' Hammer swore as he looked round the room.

He knew what was coming. Gomez would use Miranda Diaz as a shield to make him surrender. He rolled across the bed and crouched beside the bloody body of Manuel. If the bandits used Miranda Diaz as a shield he had to make a decision to risk her being killed or give himself over to the brutal torture the bandit would inflict on him.

'Joe,' the word was whispered.

Hammer stared with bewilderment at the supposed dead man on the floor beside him.

'Manuel! Goddamn, you're one tough old buzzard. They're bringing Miranda to use as a bargaining chip. It'll be a choice between her life or mine. Sorry, old man, there's no way out.'

As if to confirm Hammer's words a woman's scream cut short the conversation.

'Padre, I have Miranda Diaz out here. If you don't give up she will suffer the same fate as that friend of yours. Otherwise when we rush into the room she will be in front.'

Hammer looked thoughtfully at the wounded man lying beside him.

'Listen Manuel, we have one slim

chance. It amounts to a sheep's survival in a butcher's shop.'

The blood-encrusted lips twitched in what Hammer could only surmise was an attempt at a grin.

'Señor Joe . . . a man must have some dignity in death.'

It was with painful effort that Hammer managed to set his dying friend upright. He could feel the bullet in his own back grinding on bone as he worked.

A fusillade of shots blasted into the room and thudded into walls and furniture. Crouching behind the bed Hammer was safe from the flying lead.

'Padre, my patience is at an end. We are coming in. Careful you don't shoot the woman.'

Hammer looked up to see the terrified face of Miranda Diaz in the doorway. He waited till she was inside the room before calling out.

'OK, Gomez, you win. Just let the girl go free. I'll give myself up.'

Hammer stood up as he finished

speaking, his empty hands hanging by his side. The terrified woman was pushed further into the room and two bandits moved behind her.

'The gringo is unarmed,' one of them called out.

Gomez came warily into the room and eyed up the man standing on the other side of the bed.

'If he twitches, shoot,' he instructed his men.

The bandit chief could not resist grinning in triumph at his adversary as he tucked his own pistol into the wide sash around his middle. He pulled the lost pliers from his vest pocket and held them up.

'We can continue where we left off, Padre. I hope you have said your prayers, for in a while you will be screaming so much you will be unable to pray.'

'Send the girl home. She can be of no further use to you.'

'I believe she enjoys my company so much she would not want to leave me. I think also she enjoyed watching her friend Manuel wriggling as Mariano worked on him. I will not deprive her of the pleasure of watching you go through the same treatment.'

'Gomez! Gomez!' someone was shouting from outside.

Without taking his gaze from Hammer the bandit chief nodded to one of his men.

'Go see what that is.'

Before the man could obey another bandit pushed inside the room.

'Gomez, the soldiers have been sighted. They were seen along by the river.'

As all eyes turned to the speaker Hammer moved. He dropped on one knee and snatched up the gun he had hidden in the folds of the bed covers. A snapshot at Gomez caught the bandit chief in the neck. He spun round and clasped a hand to his wound. Blood spouted between his fingers. Then he moved with snakelike speed and grabbed Miranda Diaz around the waist.

Hammer had to ignore the bandit

chief for the moment as the other bandits in the room directed their fire at him. A shot hit him in the upper arm and he grunted as the impact almost spun him around. He fired instinctively and the two men facing him went down as his bullets hit home. The third man in the room threw himself back out into the corridor.

By then Gomez had his gun out and his first bullet hit Hammer in the collarbone. Hammer groaned aloud as he felt the bone shatter under the impact. He aimed his gun but held his fire as he saw the bandit chief sheltering behind Miranda. He tried to duck behind the bed but another bullet ploughed a furrow along his cheek and took away the lower part of his ear. He aimed and pulled the trigger. There was a click as the hammer fell on a used shell.

'Enough!' he shouted and stood up.

He could feel the blood from the fresh wound running down his face and into his shirt collar. Slowly he stood up, his hands empty. Gomez swung the girl to one side and sighted his pistol on the man who had caused him so much bother.

'I should have killed you that day in San Chrisobel, Priest,' he hissed, 'but Mariano stopped me. Now Mariano is dead along with many of my men. I would like to take you with me, Priest, and make your life a living hell before sending you to your God but I think you would be more bother than you are worth. I will have to finish you here.'

The shot rang out. The range was short but with his mangled hands Manuel could not hold the pistol very steady. The bullet hit Gomez in the arm. Hammer used the bed as a springboard as he launched himself across the room. He cannoned into Gomez as the bandit was turning his gun on Manuel. Both men went down and Gomez lost his grip on the pistol.

Hammer did not see Miranda fall upon the discarded pistol. He was too busy trying to pin Gomez to the floor.

Agony flared through his shoulder and arm as he tried to hold the struggling bandit. Gomez was hugely strong. He punched his opponent on the wounded side of his head and Hammer fell sideways as the agony in his face intensified. Stars exploded in his head and he had to fight a faintness that seemed intent on sucking him down into a black fog.

He grabbed Gomez around the neck and tried to tighten his grip. The man's neck was slippery from the flesh wound inflicted earlier. Hammer felt the muscular strength of the man as he battered at Hammer's arms. The wound in his shoulder and the one in his arm were taking their toll and Hammer felt his strength waning. His face was inches from the bandit chief's as they strained to kill each other.

'Die, Priest,' Gomez gritted.

Hammer felt the sharp pain as the dagger went into his side. He gasped and his grip on the bandit's neck slackened. Gomez pulled the knife free.

Hammer could not keep his strangle grip as Gomez moved to kneel on top of him. He watched helplessly as the bloodied knife was raised to his throat.

'Meet your maker, Priest.'

The bullet tore away the back of Gomez's head as Miranda Diaz pulled the trigger at point blank range. He sagged sideways. Hammer gave one last heave and the lifeless body slid to the carpet. For a long moment he stared at the distraught face of Miranda kneeling beside him.

'I am free,' she whispered and pushed the muzzle of the gun that had just killed Gomez into her mouth.

'No!'

He was too late. The gun kicked in the girl's hand and her head was jolted back. She sprawled to the floor, her lifeless hand slackening on the gun. Hammer grabbed up the weapon and turned it on the doorway. The surprised face of a bandit was staring into the room taking in the sprawled bodies. Before Hammer could fire the head disappeared.

'Gomez is dead!'

Hammer heard the cries as the news was passed along. He listened to running steps and the excited yelling. He tried to stand but had not the strength. As he sagged back to the floor he strove to keep his weapon trained on the doorway. Waves of dizziness swept over him and he sprawled on his face to lie motionless between the dead Miranda Diaz and Gomez Farias.

34

He stared up at the face hanging in the air above him.

'I think he might be conscious.'

He knew that face — Father Dominick.

'Señor Hammer.' the priest said.

Through the mists of pain another face floated into focus. It was the dead Miranda's sister, Anna. Hammer studied the face and thought he had never seen anyone so beautiful. Dark hair hung down and framed her beautiful, sculpted features. He stared up at her. She reached down and stroked his forehead. Her hand was cool and light on his head.

'Father, he is very hot.'

He was staring up at her, mesmerized by her dazzling beauty. She picked up a cloth and began to bathe his face. He tried to keep his eyes open and failed.

The darkness took him again and he floated away. The beautiful face stayed with him.

He was not sure how long it was before he could stay awake for longer than a few moments. He tried to sit up. His effort was a miserable failure. Waves of pain washed over him as his muscles tensed. His head was only raised an inch or two before he had to desist. When the pain subsided he took stock of his situation. His body felt as if it was encased in a full-length, very tightfitting corset. A man moved into his line of vision.

'Father Dominick,' he croaked.

'Be at peace my son. Your upper body is heavily bandaged,' Father Dominick said, gently putting his hand on Hammer's chest. 'You have been very ill. You have received many wounds any one of which should have killed you.'

'How long have I been here?'

'Three weeks.' The priest smiled gently. 'You are a strong man, Señor Hammer, but there were times when I thought I had lost you.'

'Father, I have committed a host of sins. I have dipped my hands in the blood of many men.'

'Hush now, child, enough of that. You had much provocation.'

'My provocation was revenge. Vengeance is mine saith the Lord. But I took it on myself to do his work. I blasphemed and thought I was the Hammer of God. Then I went to work and slew mine enemies.'

'We will talk of these things another time. Right now you must concentrate on recovery. Heal your body first. The mind will heal itself.'

A door opened and someone entered the infirmary.

'I heard voices, Father,' a female voice said.

He stared at Anna Diaz. She stood gazing down at him and his eyes ached as he drank in her beauty.

'I'm sorry,' he said to her. 'I could not save her. You were right not to trust me.'

Her eyes filled with tears. She pulled a lace handkerchief from her sleeve and held it to her face.

'You were not to blame, Señor Hammer. Manuel told us what you did.'

'Manuel!' He blinked in surprise. 'He is still alive?'

She smiled through her tears. 'The Diaz family are a hardy race. Our family came over with Cortès. We have survived worse than Gomez.'

He nodded. 'Manuel told me he was godfather to Miranda.'

'He was more than godfather — he was her uncle. My father and Manuel are brothers.'

'Dear God, did he see her die?'

'He told us. You could have not prevented it. Do not blame yourself.'

A knock on the door interrupted the conversation. Father Dominick went to the door and there was the murmur of voices.

'There is someone here wants to speak to you,' he said. Captain Calleja stepped inside and bowed to the girl.

'Señorita Diaz,' He turned to the man in the bed. 'Señor Hammer of God, it seems I owe you an apology.'

Hammer did not respond.

'In the end it was you who finished Gomez, and suffered much in doing so. Without your intervention Gomez would have slipped away and even now would be at liberty to continue with his lawless trade. Manuel Diaz informs us you slew many of Gomez's men before killing the bandit chief.'

The captain fumbled in his pocket and produced a large bronze medallion. There was a brass pin with a ribbon attached.

'My government have asked me to present this decoration for your services to our country.'

Stepping forward he bowed and placed the medal on the pillow. From inside his tunic he produced an official document.

'You are also awarded honorary citizenship of Mexico.'

He placed the papers on the bed beside the medal. Suddenly he stuck out his hand.

'It would be an honour to shake your hand, Señor Hammer.'

Awkwardly Hammer reached out and took the offered hand.

'Señorita.'

The captain bowed and was gone.

'Captain Calleja is a very proud man,' Father Dominick said. 'You stole his glory when single-handed you vanquished Gomez and his bandit gang.'

'So many dead men, Father. How am I to account to God for so much bloodshed?'

'*Is not my word like as a fire? saith the Lord: and like a hammer that breaketh the rock in pieces*,' the old man quoted. 'You were the hammer that broke the evil reign of Gomez. Think not on the deaths of those evil men but on the lives you have saved. By killing Gomez you put an end to his vile reign. Be at peace, my son. *But thou hast fulfilled the judgment of the wicked: judgment and justice take hold of thee. Thou art indeed an awful instrument of the Lord.'*

Somewhere in the monastery a bell began tolling.

'Please excuse me, Señor Hammer. That is the bell for evening mass.'

Left alone with the girl Hammer lay with his eyes half-closed watching her. He was remembering their last meeting. That fierce passionate kiss had stayed with him.

'Why do you visit me?' he asked abruptly.

For long steady moments she gazed at him. He began to believe his question had offended her.

'I am the elder daughter of Eugene Diaz,' she began. 'My father wanted me to marry someone rich and noble. He brought home many such suitors for me. Quickly I saw past their polished manners, their stylish dress and their smooth speech.'

She looked down at her hands then

and a slight tinge of colour crept up her face adding a delicate glow to her smoothly tanned skin.

'One day a rough peasant arrived at the ranch. I found myself strangely drawn to this person. I tried to hide my feelings by being rude. He did something no man ever dared to do before. He put his hands on my person and kissed me. I . . . I had never allowed any man that close to me before. I . . . I was strangely moved by his conduct.'

She stopped speaking and the deep crimson had invaded all of her face by now. For one brief second she raised her eyes to him, then turned and fled. Hammer turned his head and stared at the empty doorway.

'Mysterious indeed are the ways of God,' he murmured, 'and even more mysterious are those of women.'